Ms. Lucky:

Follow Your Heart

By

Misha Shorter

Dedication

In loving memory of my mom, Deborah Shorter, who was with us from 1957 to 2023.

Your love, strength, and unwavering guidance continue to light my path, even though you are no longer here. This book is dedicated to your memory — a tribute to the lessons you taught me and the love you gave so freely.

You will forever be my inspiration and my heart.

Acknowledgments

First and foremost, I want to express my deepest gratitude to my mom and dad. Without your love, patience, encouragement, or guidance, this book would not exist.

To Samantha Urias for your proofreading and edits.

Michelle Parker for being my shoulder to cry on when things got hard, and so many others who gave me ideas and names to add thank you. Your insights and kindness shaped this novel in more ways than I can say.

I am forever grateful to my agent Bruce, who supported me throughout the process of everything and then some. Iris and the crew of editors. Steinbeck Publishing for believing in this story and helping me bring it to life.

Your expertise and dedication have been invaluable.

To my readers and those who have supported my writing journey, thank you for your enthusiasm and faith in my words. This book is as much yours as it is mine.

Finally, I dedicate this acknowledgment to my mother, Deborah Shorter. Her love, strength, and spirit continue to inspire me every day. Though she is no longer with us, her presence is felt in every word I write.

Thank you all for making this dream a reality.

About the Author

Misha Shorter is an author, photographer, and dedicated mother of six boys. Alongside her creative pursuits, she works full-time as a Team Leader at the Texas Challenge Academy in Eagle Lake, Texas.

A self-proclaimed hopeless romantic, Misha channels her passion for love stories into her writing, crafting compelling tales of romance. She has been writing since 2012 and published the first installment of her four-part novel series, *Ms. Lucky: By Any Means Necessary*, in May 2019.

Through her work, Misha continues to inspire readers with her vivid imagination and heartfelt storytelling.

Table of Contents

Chapter 1

Quality Time

They left the hotel and ended up going to get a bite to eat. "Where would you like to eat?" Tim asks.

"I have a taste for fish." Julissa says.

So, Tim thought of going to a food truck a little ways down the highway, called FishN'More. He had eaten there before, and he knew the food was great!

They both ordered a fish plate. Two big pieces of fish, fries, and a roll. They decided to sit outside. The weather was kind of nice. There were a few tablesoutside, so they decided to sit and eat out there.

They talk for a bit, while still eating their food, and then Tim gets a phone call andwalks away pretty fast. Julissa started thinking. It must be important.

He then comes back and tells her, he has something very important to take care of and that they need to go ahead and get on back.

She said, "Okay," and gets up. They walk back to his car and drive on back to hersuite. He hugs and kisses her on the cheek and then says, "I will explain everything later. I promise."

She gets out and he drives off. She walks inside and up to her suite. As she begins to go in, she sees a young girl sitting in the hallway crying, so she goes to see whatis wrong with her — hoping to comfort her.

She calmly walks up to her and says, "Hey, are you okay? Is there anything I cando?"

The girl rudely snaps at her and says, "Do I look okay?"

Julissa almost cursed the girl out, but instead, she says, "I was just checking on you, but if you're going to have an attitude, I can go!" Julissa says.

"I am so sorry. Honestly, I didn't mean it that way, girl. My boyfriend and I just broke up! He has been cheating on me with my cousin for months, and I just foundout she is pregnant because of him. She is 6 weeks going! It was a whole ordeal."

"Oh, no. That is so messed up. Your cousin. Oh, my. How dare her!" Julissa says, then continues, "How did you find out?"

"Well, I probably would have never found out, but he had to tell me once thefamily announced she was pregnant." She says.

"Okay, next question. Where is he now?" Asked Julissa.

"He is in our suite." She says. "That is the last time I saw him. I'm sure he didn't goanywhere, yet. Before all this happened, he was talking about going out."

"And why are you out here? Julissa asks, "He needs to be the one out here! That nigga ain't worth shit. You need to go find you a real man. I am glad you are not theone who got pregnant! Girl, I know it will be hard, but you can move on with your life." Julissa encourages the other girl.

1

"Well, I already have a son with him. He is two. His 3rd birthday is tomorrow. We have a party set up for him and everything. How am I going to do that?" She asks. "Well, you seem like a great mommy. I'm sure you are, too. But you are going to have to be strong for him. Don't cancel. If that is what you were thinking. Just give him thebest day ever. And then, if you need some time, then take some, but don't spoil the little man's day!! He has nothing to do with this situation." Julissa says.

"As far as cheating, though, it seems like a lot of that is going on around here." SaysJulissa.

"What do you mean?" She asked.

"Oh, I just recently was dumped too, girl, so I can feel ya pain." Says Julissa

"Huh." She says. "As beautiful as you are?"

"Girl, let me tell you something. These days it doesn't even matter what we looklike. A nigga will cheat, even though mine didn't, but that is another totally different conversation. But with your situation, you are a gorgeous girl, and you see whatjust happened to you. And I'm sure it has been happening right in front of you, too! These niggas missing out though. One day, they're gonna have to recognize us!! Theycan't keep on doing this, and getting away with it!!"

"Well, now, since you are trying to get in my business, Hi, I am Julissa Lucky form116B, and you are?" She asked.

"Paulina Shaft." She says.

"Well, it has been nice meeting you, Miss Shaft! Hold on, Shaft?" She asks

"Shaft? Really? I am kin to the Shafts, off of Ridley, And Anderson St. on the otherside of town." Julissa says.

"Yes, Denise and Irwin Shaft are my mom and dad." Says Paulina.

"Okay, then. We are family!! Nice to meet you. Now, back to the matter at hand.

So, did he kick you out or did you go willingly?" Asked Julissa.

"No, I left on my own. I just didn't get very far before I broke down right here inthis hallway. Then you showed up, and here we are." Paulina says

"How about you come to my suite? I am sure you can relax there better than outhere." Julissa says.

"Okay, that sounds great. I'll give him time to leave the suite, and then I will gethis things and put them in some bags and sit them out like trash." She says.

"Now you are talking, my new friend and/or family, whatever you prefer. Maybe you should push him a littlefaster." Says Julissa. "We need to go. I am right down the hall."

Paulina quickly gets up and follows Julissa to her suite.They get to the room and Paulina sits down on the sofa.

"Would you like a drink?" Asked Julissa.

"Sure, I will take a soda or water. Whatever, really it doesn't matter." Paulina says,"Okay, sweetie, but all I have is water, wine, and some pineapple juice. I had somevodka but my brother drank it the other day, when he came by." Says Julissa. "I amgoing to grab myself a glass of wine. It has been a very crazy day for me."

"I will take a bottle of water." Paulina nods to Julissa.

"Alright, here." Julissa hands her the water. "You go, because you probably do not need anything else to drink. You look like you've had quite a bit already!" Julissa assumes.

"I am not drunk if that is what you are implying." Says Paulina "Yes, I have had a few drinks, but wouldn't anyone that just got the news I've just found out?"

"Well, you could have fooled me. Looking like a lost puppy out there in the hall, crying over this dude." Says Julissa.

"I was not crying because I still wanted him. I was crying because of the situation. I mean, girl, my cousin, really?" Says Paulina. "This is going to really ruin our relationship, because I trusted her. Fuck him. I already was about to dump him, but my cousin is family. I really need to do a lot of thinking about that. She overstepped this time."

Julissa says, "I think you need to try to fix your relationship with your cousin, but forget him."

"I'm sure he has left by now. I am going to try to go back to my suite." She says, as she gets up and walks towards the door, "but thank you… for being such a sweet neighbor, and now, I know you are also my family. I will be sure to tell my mom and dad I ran into you, or at least that you are Mama Lucky's daughter." Paulina smiles as she says her goodbyes.

"Yes, you be sure to do that, and I will talk to my mom about it, too." Julissa says, "Maybe sometime soon, we can all get together. Maybe have a gathering or something."

"Oh, we would love that, but I will definitely be in touch. Here is my number. Please add me." She says

Julissa then picks up her phone off the coffee table and begins to type as Paulina says the number out loud for her.

Paulina says "It is   706-456-8754."

"So, you said '706-456-8754?'" Asked Julissa.

"That's right." Says Paulina.

"Once you get back in the suite, shoot me a text. I want to make sure he is gone, or I might have to have a friend of mine make him leave. He can't stand a nigga like that." Says Julissa.

"Okay, sure thing. I will." She says as she opens the door and leaves.

After Paulina leaves, Julissa sits down on the sofa and starts thinking, "Damn, I wonder what was so important that Tim had to cut our date or whatever it was so short?" She guessed they could talk about it tomorrow or sometime soon.

"Anyways, it is still early. It is really early in fact. It is only 9pm, and I am at home. This was crazy." She thought out loud to herself. "I am not sure what he is doing, and considering it has nothing to do with me, but I am going to go out!"

She calls her friend, Jennifer, and of course, she does not answer the first time. Julissa calls her about three more times, and still no answer. She decided to give her a few minutes. She goes to the restroom and sits down to do her business. While she was in there, she could hear the phone ringing, but she was still not finished.

3

Realizing it must be that wine, she sits a little longer, before wiping and getting up. Meanwhile, the phone is ringing and ringing, but she is still finishing up in the bathroom, so she ignores it. She checks her phone to see who called her, and sees an unfamiliar number. Thinking it might be Jenn calling her back, she gets frustrated and throws the phone down on the couch. Then after sitting and waiting on her friend to call her back, she gets a little irritated, and goes into the kitchen and pours another glass of wine. It was called Stella Rose. It was this new wine that her sister brought her. She tasted it and was instantly hooked. She brought about 4 bottles, when she went grocery shopping. She grabbed her glass, and turned on some music. A few minutes later the phone rings again and it is finally Jennifer.

She answers with, "Damn, I was about to send out a search party for your ass. You know I was starting to worry. You never make me wait so long to hear back from you. I do not care what you were particularly doing, but why didn't you answer."

"Girl, I was in the shower, and my music was so loud, I couldn't hear the phone. I am so sorry I worried you, but what's up?" Asked Jennifer.

"Nothing really, boo." Julissa says, "I just got dropped off by Tim, a little while ago, and it was so early I decided I wanted to go out, which is why I called to see if you would like to go also?" She asked.

"Tim? Wait, what? Who the hell is Tim? It seems as if we do need to link up, sis. I have obviously missed a lot while you were away." Asked Jennifer.

"Obviously." Says Julissa.

"So, first things first." She says, "What happened to that fine ass, Dennis?"

"Oh, we broke up a few weeks ago." Says Julissa.

"Broke up? Damn, what happened? This better be a damn good explanation 'cause y'all were doing so good, and baby boy was fine!" Asked Jennifer.

"Well, you remember everything I told you I had to do in order to get that VP position, yeah?" Asked Julissa.

"Yes." She says. "Everything was going great for a couple of months, and then all of a sudden, Mr. Prince started getting pushy and wanted me to do more. Had me doing extra stuff to get Dennis to sign with the company. I had to keep telling him one lie after another to make One Take look better to him." She said. "I lied so much that it started to feel like a true story I was telling every time. Anyways to make a long story short Mr. Prince started getting even more pushy and wanting Dennis to sign with the company quicker. Dennis was dragging his feet, and wasn't completely sure at first. I had to do everything in my power including making him trust me to get him to sign on. Honestly. At first it was just a job, but then we actually fell in love with each other and that changed the rules. Even though there were none."

"Well, once I finally got Dennis to sign. Mr. Prince was so excited that he invited Dennis to a welcome lunch with the VP (myself) and himself. Of course, I couldn't get out of it. That day was the worst day of my freaking life. Dennis shows up and realizes I worked for One Take and he just went ballistic. He called me every name you could think of and he literally refused to work with me. He said I betrayed him, called me another bitch, and then just left pretty pissed." Julissa explained "So, baby boy is still gonna work with the company?" Asked Jennifer.

"Yes. He just said that he did not want to work with me directly. Any kind ofbusiness stuff, Mr. Prince would have to be there." Says Julissa.

"Okay, well there still may be a chance for you two!" She says excitedly. "Oh, that isright, there is now a Tim in the equation? Okay, now, who is this Tim guy you speaking of?" Asked Jennifer.

"Doesn't matter anyway, because I don't want him." Julissa says.

"Well, okay, now. I guess this is the part where Tim comes into the story?" She asks.

"Yes, girl, he is an old boyfriend that was already in town for a few days. A few days before that happened he had come to my mom's to see me. Something my mom setup. Anyways, it just so happened that he had gotten a suite in the hotel where I was staying. However, after Dennis and I fell out, I ran back into Tim, and we have beenseeing each other ever since." Says Julissa.

"OMG, your life has basically been one big ass soap opera, girl. Nothing exciting ever happens like this for me." Says Jennifer. "I need some excitement of my own."

"You call this exciting? Girl, you need to really get some business, because you obviously have nothing going on in yours." Says Julissa.

"That is what I just said." She says, "You need to listen better."

"Okay, so is that it? Is that all that happened? He hasn't even come around trying toget you back?" Jennifer asks "So just like that, you and Dennis are completely done?"

"Yes. I would be the happiest girl in the world, if I never saw him again. Of course, that cannot happen due to the fact that I'm his boss! Damn! I get to see his ass every day." Julissa sighs as she laments her situation.

"Okay, now that this is all out, did you say something about going out?" AskedJennifer.

"Yes, Tim had some business to attend to so he dropped me off at my suite. Comeon by, and we can go to that new spot in downtown, Atlanta, called Club Precise." Says Julissa.

"Okay, that sounds great! Let me get dressed, and I will call you once I am on myway."

"I will be here and ready once you get here." Says Julissa.

"Okay, boo." Says Jennifer, as she hangs up the phone.

Julissa goes into her bedroom and grabs a cute skirt, and shirt to go with it. She jumps into the shower and takes a quick one, and jumps right on out and wraps her towel around her. She then grabs the outfit laid out on her bed. Realizing she had forgotten her bra and panties, she then goes to her dresser drawer and grabs a blacklace set. She drives herself off completely, and then slides on her panties first and then the bra. She put on the red blouse, and a Black leather skirt that she had already picked out. She also grabs some thigh high boots and puts them on and then goes to the living room to wait for Jennifer to arrive.

After about 15 more minutes Jennifer calls and says she is on her way. Looking at the time, it is now 10:00 P.M. Julissa quickly goes to the kitchen and pours herself another glass of Stella Rose, and sits back down on the sofa, and says "Alexa, play Keri Hilson's 'Pretty Girl Rock', so I can get into clubbing mood." Still thinking about Timhaving to leave suddenly, but she was not going to let him dim her mood. So, she started singing to the song in her mind, easily distracted. Jennifer calls again and tells Julissa she is downstairs.

Julissa says "Well, park your car and come up here! I am ready but I thought wewould have a drink before we head out."

"Great! What is your suite number?" Asked Jennifer.

"116B on the 6th floor." Julissa says.

"Okay. I will be right up." Jennifer says.

"Great. See you soon." Says Julissa.

A few minutes later, Jennifer knocks and Julissa yells to let her know to come in. "It's open."

Jennifer comes in, and goes straight to the kitchen looking in the fridge forsomething to drink, to take a few shots.

"Where is the drank at, sis? I need a shot." Says Jennifer.

"A shot of what?" Julissa asks. "Because all I have is wine right now."

"Oh, man, really? That's it? Did you really think I came up here to have a drink of wine? You know me way better than that, Liss! I need a shot of some hard liquor. Today was a pretty hectic day. You really want me to go out and have to buy my own drinks?" She says "Wow! You really have been distracted by love or I just don't know what else, girl. Let's get out of here. I am so ready to go now. It hasbeen a minute since you and I had a great time out in the "A"."

"I have really missed you, girl." Says Julissa, trying to gather her wits but failing to do so and laughing hard. "I am ready now,too. I just need to grab a light jacket and we can be out the door."

"Okay. Can I get one also? Jennifer asked, "It was a bit chilly when I got out of mycar. I just didn't want to go back in and get one. Girl, you know you got plenty of crap in that closet." Says Jennifer.

"Girl, come on in here and find you one to match your outfit." Julissa says. "I amthinking of a blue jean." Julissa suggests.

They both walk into the bedroom. Julissa grabs a thin leather jacket, and Jennifer aBlue jean jacket to try to match with her jeans she is wearing. Fitting oh-so tight, and just right.

They then leave the suite and get on the elevator. But are interrupted, because as soon as the elevator dooropens, Dennis is there. "We must have opened the door back open?" Julissa thought.

Of course, he has something to say. He says "Hey, where are you two going,looking all delicious?"

"None of your damn business!!" Julissa says, with a stinky attitude.

Dennis quickly says, "Well, excuse me, Miss Attitude! I was just asking. You two out here looking prettier than a mutha'. A nigga can't be nice? Damn! You do not haveto be so rude. I thought we were done with all that. It was days ago. I don't know about you, but I try not to hold grudges for too long. Negativity is bad for your health."

"Hi, Dennis." Jennifer quickly says to try to calm things down a bit.

"Oh, hi, there." He says, "You must be the best friend. I have heard a lot about you,but none of how beautiful you are!" He says as he looks in Julissa's direction to try to get a rise out of her, but he gets nothing from her.

They make it to the lobby, and they all get off. They walk outside, and Big Joe iswaiting in the car for Dennis.

"Would y'all like to take a shot with us? Just one. I see y'all are going out. Why notstart early. I am sure Julissa only had some wine in the fridge."

"Wow… that is exactly right." Says Jennifer. "Sure, I would. What you got?"

"I got vodka, and Hennessey. Which one would you like, Brown or White?" Heasked.

"Hi, ladies." Says Big Joe.

"Hey, friend. How are you tonight?" Asked Julissa.

"Blessed. It's been a pretty good day. How about you two? He asked.

"Oh, it's been a great day for me." Says Jennifer.

"Ms. Lucky, how about you?" He asked, "Who is your friend?"

"Oh, my day was kinda crazy, but nothing I couldn't handle. Thanks for asking. Youare such a gentleman." She says, looking over at Dennis.

She just kept looking at him like he better stop."So, what's your name, gorgeous? Asks Dennis.

"Jennifer Avila." She says.

"Oh, okay, Miss Jennifer. Very nice to meet you." He says.

"Girl, stop telling him all your business!" Says Julissa. "He doesn't need to knowanything else." Says Julissa with a very prissy attitude. "Why are you tryna pushup on my friend?"

"I'm not. I am just trying to get to know her. That is all." He says.

"Why are you talking to him, anyways? Asked Julissa. "He is the enemy." She says.

"Enemy? Wow. That is truly what you think of me? Even though you were the onemisleading me, but, I'm the one that is wrong? Oh my gosh, girl. You have gotten itall figured out, don't you? Nah, you don't, but it's cool. I am going to leave you alone and let you cool down. I've obviously struck a nerve, even though it shouldbe the other way around." He says in response to Julissa's harsh attitude.

"Well, I didn't want to be rude."

Jennifer looks at her friend and says, "You really are being rude, Lissa."

"We are not particularly talking right now. You are supposed to have my side." Says Julissa "He has no reason speaking to me outside the office."

"Well, I did speak to you. I was trying to get over this little ordeal that you caused,and we start over, but you keep giving me the cold shoulder." He says.

"Dennis, you and I are done! No, I don't want you back! You know I like someoneelse, anyways. So, I wish you would just stop. Come on, Jenn. Let's go." Says Julissa. "I do not have any more time for his shenanigans. We have somewhere to be Dennis. Now, boy, bye." Julissa says.

"I asked you that already." Dennis says.

"Yes, and I ignored that question, because you did not need to know. It's none ofyour concern." Says Julissa, while waving her hand in a dismissive manner as she walks away. "Bye, Big Joe." She directs at the other man.

"Well, Miss Jennifer, where are you two going all jazzed up? He asks again.

"I would tell you, but I am sure that Julissa would be really pissed at me. So, I amnot going to tell you anything else. This conversation ends here. Goodnight, Dennis" Says Jennifer as she walks off a little behind Julissa.

Julissa then screams back to Jennifer. "Let's go. He is just trying to get you to tellhim where we are going."

"I'm coming. I'm coming. Damn! I will meet you in the car. I just unlocked it. She says as she presses for it to unlock remotely.

"Bye, Dennis. It was nice to meet you, but I have to go." Says Jennifer. "You musthave really pissed Julissa off."

Jennifer gets in the driver's seat, and starts the car, and drives off towards the club. They drive about 10 minutes before they finally get there. The sign says Club Precise. It's all lit up, and the lights are in Red. You couldn't miss this place if youtried. The building was big. I could imagine what it looked like on the inside.

Jennifer and Julissa looked at their faces to make sure their make-up was good. Once they are agreed they both get out of the car. They walk up to get in line and the bouncer motions for them to come up front. Once they get up front, the bounceropens the chain and lets them go straight into the V.I.P. section. They sit down, and their waitress walks up and asks them what they would like to drink. Julissa orders a crown on the rocks, while Jennifer orders two shots of tequila. "Clearly, she was notgonna drive us back home." Julissa thought.

After a few minutes, the waitress arrives with their drinks. Jennifer quickly chugsboth shots and then orders a few more.

"Girl, please, slow down." Says Julissa.

They both watched their surroundings for a bit, as Julissa sips her crown, andJennifer eats the nuts on the table.

"Do not need any of those hating ass females coming up here starting some shitand trying to be petty." Says Jennifer.

"Wow, there is a pretty big crowd in here. I am sure you will find plenty of ballersin here tonight, Jenn." Says Julissa.

"I know, right?" Says Jennifer. "It's some fine ass men in here, but nothing evenremotely fine ass that nigga you just seriously dissed at the hotel."

"Shut up, Jennifer! I already explained that situation to you." Says Julissa.

"Oh, I am sure you're still masturbating to the memory of that D." Says Jennifer."Don't lie. I know he was packing, and put it down in the bedroom."

"Damn, you are talking too loud." Says Julissa "I can't deal with you." Though her words sound harsh to anyone else, but Jennifer can see the bigass grin on her face.

"Oh, I can see it all over your face, boo. You still want that D!! Wit' yo' nasty ass."

Says Jennifer.

"There is way more to a man than the way he looks." Says Julissa.

"Maybe you, miss lady, but for me he better be fine. If he is ugly, I won't even step close to him." says Jennifer.

"That is a really shallow thing to say, but some guys can be fine as aged wine, and havethe mind of a pea. So, you better be careful what you wish for." Says Julissa. "Well, once you get past the exterior what do you look for?"

"I look at how he is dressed." Jenifer says.

"That is an important thing. He has got to know how to dress. Okay, I am with youon that one. What is next?" Asked Julissa.

"Nice ass" Says Jennifer.

"Oh my gosh. There you go again. What does a man's butt have to do with the wayhe treats you?" Julissa asks.

"Absolutely nothing. I just want it to be kinda thick and toned."

"Anyways, are you interested in any guys you have seen yet?" Asked Julissa.

"Yes, Lissa. I see a few, in here, in fact, that I might ask to buy me a drink." Says Jennifer. She continues to look around and then towards Julissa, saying carefully. "Don't trip, but Mr. From-Whom-You-Don't-Want just walked in here."

Julissa looks directly at him and says, "What is he doing here? You told him wherewe were going didn't you?" Julissa quickly assumed.

"No, I did not tell him, because I knew you would be mad at me." Says Jennifer.

"Well, then what is he doing here? Julissa asked.

"Hell. I don't know. Maybe he just heard about the opening tonight and came justlike us." Says Jennifer.

"Hopefully he doesn't bother me." Says Julissa, "I don't feel like dealing with himanymore."

She then looks away from Dennis and right into Tim's hazel eyes, as he is walkingby.

"Oh, hey beautiful. What are you doing here? He asked.

"I have a better question. Did you break off our date to come here? Julissa asks.

"Of course not, babe. I had to go and take care of some other business, but then myboy invited me out to his club to help him with some things. So, I said, sure. I figured you were home, getting some rest." Tim says.

"Well, it was pretty early when you dropped me off, so I called my girl. Told her weneeded to check out this new club. So, here we are."

"By the way, how did you two get in the V.I.P. section?" Tim asked.

"Oh, they let us in for free, and sat us here in the V.I.P. It was pretty cool. Weactually didn't have to wait in line like everyone else. Once we got inside, the bouncer said we didn't deserve to sit anywhere else but here. So, there you go.Where are you sitting?"

"I am also in V.I.P. but that's because the owner is my homeboy. I wasn't sure just how long your money was but these tables are very pricey. These tables run at least300 dollars, and you have to buy at least one bottle." Tim explains "Don't worry though, I am sure if the bouncer set you here, he planned on paying for the table too."

"Oh, damn." Says Jennifer. "We might need to go ask, dude."

"I am going to go back to my table." Says Tim. "I will see you a little later, babe. Goahead and enjoy yourself."

Tim walked away and then the bouncer came over and sat down with them. "Hey, are we going to have to pay for this table? We just heard it costs a prettypenny to sit here and we do not have enough to cover it." Ask Julissa.

"No, it will be taken care of. We just wanted to sit the flyest ladies at our best tabletonight. You ladies fit the profile so there you go." Says the bouncer.

"Well… that is good to know. We can have some fun now." Says Julissa.

"Yeah, girl. I was kind of worried thinking we were going to have to pay for thistable. Oh, I got it, but I'm not trying to pay for it." Says Jennifer.

"Girl, I hear you. Me neither. My money is for other things." Julissa says.

"Anyways, let's go and dance. I like this song." Says Jennifer.

"I'm good. I will sit this one out. You go ahead." Says Julissa. "I'm about to getanother drink."

"Yeah, I see you were over there, babysitting the first one." Jennifer says.

"Girl, so. I don't want to be laid out over the toilet later, throwing up from drinkingtoo much. Plus, you know I've always been a slow sipper. I am in no hurry to haveto buy another drink. Just need my li'l buzz and I'm good to go."

She says.

Jennifer gets up and goes onto the dance floor.

Julissa walks up to the bar, because the waitress must have gotten lost. She hadn't come back at all. She stands there for a second, because there were people already standing in line waiting for their drinks. She finally gets up to the bar and orders another crown and coke, on the rocks of course. After a few more minutes the handsome bartender says that will be 8 bucks. Julissa gives him her card, and he puts it in the machine, gives it back, and then hands her the drink. She said "Thankyou and walked away and back to her table.

The bouncer comes back and asks, "Did you need anything, and where is yourfriend?"

She then pointed on the dance floor, because that was exactly where Jennifer was — still dancing.

"That tequila got her out there, actin' out." Julissa says.

"Well, damn, I just bought my own drink, and now you wanna show back up. I'mgood though. Just gonna drink my drink and look around a bit." She says.

"Oh, okay. Well, I am going to go back to my post, outside. I should be done out therein about an hour. I'll be back here to join you two then." He says.

"Uh, Okay." Says Julissa, looking all crazy. "He must think we are single." Shethought to herself.

10

"Thanks, but I will be fine." Says Julissa.

Jennifer then comes back to the table and dives back into her seat. "Man, I amtired." She says "That dude didn't want to let me go."

"Yeah, I saw you two over there getting it in. You had some good moves, girl. Ididn't know you could dance like that. I didn't think you had any rhythm." SaysJulissa with a big ass grin on her face.

"Forget you, girl. I can dance. Actually, I have been practicing, so I got this." Jennifersays.

"Yeah, yeah. I could see. Go, girl! That dude was feeling it too. He looked reallyinterested." Says Julissa.

"Well, I am gonna let the fine specimen of a man buy me a drink. See you in afew." Says Jennifer.

"Okay, bye." Says Julissa.

Jennifer walks away towards the bar, and a little while later, he did just that. He bought her a drink. Julissa watched as she came back with her drink and all the while thinking, "Ihave got a man in here and I still had to buy my own drink. Crazy."

And not even a moment later, Tim comes back to the table, and asks Julissa, if she needed anything? She says "Well, where were you when I was at the bar, buying my own drink a few minutesago?" Asked Julissa.

"Oh, we were in the back, counting money. There is a nice crowd in here tonight."

Says Tim.

"Yes, there are quite a few people here. Well, now it's getting late. I think I amabout to go on home." Says Julissa.

"Why, baby? I am free now. You don't want to dance with your man for a fewsongs, first?" Asked Tim.

"Okay, sure, baby. I'll dance with you. We can finish out our date night. I'd lovethat." She says.

They walked towards the dance floor, and began to slow dance. Julissa is lookingat Tim, and he is looking at her.

"Damn, baby, you are working that outfit." He says "I am going to have to take youout, a lot more often."

"I would certainly like that." Says Julissa.

Julissa then suddenly turns around and starts grinding on him, getting him all excited in places he could not control. He was really feeling her moves and started to grind back. She then gets excited and turns back around and they are undressingeach other with their eyes. Thinking about what was going to happen once they gotback to the suite.

They danced for a little while longer, and then Tim said "Baby, you ready to go?"

"Yes, I am." She says. "That drink went right through me. I am feeling a little too good right now, babe."

Jennifer then walks over to where they are and says, "Hi, Tim, right?"

"Yes. That would be me." Tim says.

"It's nice to meet you. I'm Julissa's co-worker, Jennifer." She says.

"Nice to meet you, too." Says Tim.

"Listen, Jenn. I am going to go home with Tim. We will pass you on the wayhome, so let us know if you need to ride with us?" Says Julissa.

"Did you forget, Liss? I drove us." She says.

"Oh, yeah, I know you drove here, but there is no way I am letting you drive back,or I can drive your car, and Tim will follow us." Says Julissa.

"Oh, no, I want to stay a bit longer. I am not ready to go just yet. I will get an Uber,or have my new friend take me home." Says Jennifer.

"I don't know about all that, Jennifer. You don't even know him that well." SaysJulissa.

"Oh, babe. Don't worry about it. I will have my boy keep an eye out to make sureshe is okay." Tim says.

"Are you sure you can trust your boy? You know how niggas change up, when theygot the upper hand!" She says "I mean that is my friend. I will never forgive myselfif something were to happen to her."

"Oh, no. Not this nigga. He doesn't even drink. I know he will watch her back. Hehas sisters. He would never let a woman be disrespected, or hurt." He says "I willgo find him and point her out, so he will take care of her."

"Alright then, babe. If you trust him then I guess it's okay. Thank him for me." Shesays, "Because she has been drinking quite a bit, and I don't want any of these jerksin here, try to take advantage of her."

"He will not let anything like that happen to her. Not on his watch." Says Tim.

Tim then leaves and goes to find and talk to his friend, and while he is gone, Julissasits down to wait, because she is a bit tipsy herself.

Jennifer walks off with the guy she was dancing with, and goes to sit in the side barlounge in the back of the club in another, more secluded, V.I.P. section.

Tim comes back and motions for Julissa to get up. Grabs her by the hand. He says "Are you ready, baby? She is in good hands and will be taken care of. He said they will keep an eye out for her until she leaves. Also, he told me to tell you that there are cameras all over the club. Nowhere they can't see." He says "By the way, his name is Fabian Fletcher. Please go and say goodbye to your girl, and make sure sheknows his name."

"Okay, babe. I will be right back." She says as she goes to say goodbye to Jennifer. A few minutes later Julissa returns and says, "I am feeling really tired now."No problem, babe. Then let's go."

They leave the club and go back to her suite. They begin kissing and enjoyingevery inch of each other, then Julissa excuses herself to go to the restroom.

While in the restroom, Julissa is throwing up all the liquor she drank. She is therefor quite some time. Once she comes out, Tim is crashed out on the couch.

Feeling kind of disappointed, but actually a little relieved, she grabs a blanket from her closet, and lays it slowly over him, trying not to wake him, and curls up next to him. She forgot she had to go into work for a bit tomorrow. She looks at the clock and itis damn near 12 A.M. She then hugs her man and closes her eyes and instantly falls asleep.

Meanwhile, at the club. Once Julissa and Tim leave, most of the other people havealready left. There are only a few people left.

Jennifer and her new friend Corey, began to drink a little more and one thing led toanother and Corey pulled Jennifer in close and kissed her. He must have come on alittle too strong, because Jennifer moved away.

The owner, Mr. Fletcher then comes up to Corey, pulls him to the side and says "Hey, I am about to go do a quick money drop. Keep an eye on her for me, please. Her friend would kill me if something happened to her."

"Okay, bro. No problem. She is in good hands." Says Corey.

"Okay. I'll be right back." He walks out the door, and out back, and leaves in his rangerover.

Back on the inside Corey keeps trying to put his hands under Jennifer's shirt, andshe keeps pushing his hands away.

She then says, "Where did your boy go? I thought he was supposed to make sure Iwas good!"

"Oh, yeah he had to make a run, real quick. Said he will be right back." "Well, I am ready to go home. I am going to call my girl, Julissa." She says.

"What? No, I will take you home." He says.

"No, I am gonna call my friend." She says again.

He then grabs her phone and puts it down his pants and says "You still want it to come and get it?" Jennifer feeling a li'l drunk and woozy says, "Yes, I need my phone.Just give it to me. Why must you play games? I am not putting my hands down your pants. That is crazy."

"No. You need to come get it. If you want it bad enough, don't be a punk. Come getit." He teases.

She then walks over to him and puts her hands down towards his pants and he grabs her and pulls her on top of him. He begins to kiss her. This time tonguing herdown forcefully. She tries to pull away from him, but he holds her tight. She then slaps him, and tries to get out of his grasp, but he won't let her. Calls her a bitch, and says, "Why did you hit me?"

"Because you were holding me too tight. I figured it was the only way to make youlet go." She says.

"Well, that was a very big mistake", and slaps her back. She falls onto the table andit breaks. She quickly grabs her arm and yells, "You didn't have to slap me, much less, so hard. You. Asshole. I think you broke my arm. It hurts really bad!!" She cries.

"Oh, shit, really?" Asks Corey. "I just wanted to get back at you. Didn't realize, I hadhit you that hard. Damn, do you need to go to the hospital, or some shit?"

"I'm not sure, but my damn arm is killing me." She says.

"Come on here, girl. I am taking you." He says.

13

"Give me my phone. I need to call Julissa." She says. They began to walk towards the door.

Just then, Fabian walks back in and says "What the f*** happened here? Somebody better start talking! Why is she holding her arm, Corey?"

"It was an accident. I am sorry, Boss." Says Corey.

"Accident? What accident?" As he looks to the floor to see the glass everywhere from the table. "Again. What happened to her arm?" He asks.

"We have to go, Boss. I will explain everything to you later." Says Corey.

"Where?" Asks Fabian.

"The hospital. She said her arm is hurting pretty bad. I need to make sure it is okay. It might be broken." He says as they walk out the door.

As they are driving, Jennifer calls Julissa and wakes her up. She answers with a low toned, "Hello, Jenn, are you okay?" "Not, exactly. I am on my way to the hospital."

"Hospital? What? Why? Are you alright? Never mind. I am on my way. You can explain when I get there." As she hangs up.

They make it to the hospital, and Jennifer gets out and walks in. Corey runs behind her, and helps her inside. They speak with the receptionist and she signs some papers. She sits down and wait to be called.

Julissa walks in and wonders why this has happened, while she motions for Corey to move out of the seat next to Jennifer.

"What happened, Jenn?"

She starts to explain and all of a sudden, they call her name, and she has to go to see the doctor.

She sees the doctor, and he examines her. "You only have a sprain. She will be in a sling for a few weeks and it should be better by then." Says Doctor Norman.

She comes back about an hour later, and leaves with Julissa. They get into the car. She now explains to her what really happened.

"What? He what? Slapped you? Oh, this is BS. You need to report him!" She says "Well, I did slap him first, and he did apologize, so I am going to leave it alone." She says.

"Yes, you did but he ain't a real man, hitting a woman." Julissa says, "But that is another conversation. We can revisit this later. Let's get you home."

They drive on to Jennifer's place. She makes sure she gets inside safe and sound then she heads back to her own home. Looking at the clock once she gets in her suite. It is 2 A.M. Knowing she needs to get up in a few hours, she lays back next to Tim and goes back to sleep.

Chapter 2

The Promotion

Julissa woke up around 5:15 A.M. Surprisingly she didn't wake Tim up. Not sure how they slept on the couch all night, but they did. She gets up and goes to take a shower. While in the shower, she lets the water run down her back. It is so hot, it feels like a massage. She was taking her time there because she didn't have to go intoday until 7 A.M. or at least that is what time she tries to make it into the office. She washes the rest of her body, gets out, grabs her towel, and dries off. By this time she can smell coffee brewing. Knowing damn sure that she didn't start the coffee, she figured Tim must be up. She walks to the kitchen, and Tim is buck naked pouring two cups of hot coffee. He cannot see her because his back is turned toward her. She then quietly turns around and walks back into the bedroom. She goes to the closest to pick out something to wear for the day.

She decides on some dressy khaki slacks, and a cute Black top with a black belt. She sits down on the bed and just begins to think about life and the things that havebeen happening to her. Thinking things like, if she really even want to start something new right now? Does she still want to see if she and Dennis have a chance? Or is she even ready to deal with this situation, and all that will come with it? She quickly comes back to reality and figures out that yes, she is definitely ready for this situation and see where her and Tim could lead. Dennis is old news.

She then checks her phone and realizes she has been daydreaming for quite a whileso she jumps up, goes to her closet, and grabs some low heel boots, and sits down on the bed to put them on.

She walks into the living room and Tim is up watching TV with a cup of coffee. Hehands her her cup as she walks by. He also realizes that she is about to be late. Hehad already put it in her Yeti. She gives him a kiss, and he gets up to hug her goodbye.

She says, "I will see you later, right? He agrees and says "Call me when you get abreak. I will be at my suite, most likely"

"That sounds good. I will be sure to give you a call." She says while walking outthe door.

"Okay. Bye." He says as the door closes behind her.

Julissa is walking towards the elevator, and as she passed Dennis's suite she hoped he didn't come out. Fortunately he didn't. Once she got to the elevator andthe door was about to close, guess who grabs the door and it comes back open.

Dennis!

"Hey beautiful. How are you this lovely Monday morning?" He asks.

"Why must you talk to me outside the office?" Asked Julissa "I told you we areover."

"Well, can a brotha be nice and speak?" Asked Dennis.

"I guess. I am doing okay. Running a little late." She says.

"Me too. Especially if you are running late. I know I am." He says.

Julissa smirks a bit as she is about to smile.

15

Dennis catches it and says "Ooh, I'm wearing you down. Pretty soon we will becool again. I will just sit back, be patient and wait." He says.

"Boy, not even gonna happen, but you can have your thoughts about the situationall you want." Says Julissa as the elevator stops.

They get off and go their separate ways. Julissa heads on towards her car, and BigJoe is out front to pick up Dennis. They drive off and on to the office.

Julissa gets in still smiling as if Dennis said something true. She starts her car, putsit in reverse, and backs up. Put it in drive and goes to the office.

She gets to work. Finds her spot, parks her car and for some reason looks forDennis to be dropped off, but he doesn't come.

She walks inside, gets on the elevator, and goes on up to the *One Take* floor.As she reaches her floor, and the elevator opens and she is greeted with balloons, flowers, candy boxes, and her office is filled with even more. Everyone just keeps saying congratulations Ms. V.P. She walks on by her office towards Mr. Prince's office and for some reason he is not there.

She walks down the hall and asks Anna "Do you know if Mr. Prince is here, yet?"

She says, "No. I haven't seen him, but I just got here a little while ago."

Julissa quickly goes to her emails. She hadn't received anything this morning. "Well, to my knowledge he is supposed to be here this morning." Says Julissa.

"What do we need to do, Ms. Lucky?" Jerome asks.

"Just get on your computers and find something to do till I give you all further instructions." She says. "I'll go do the same. If anyone needs me that is where Iwill be."

Just as she was walking back to her office Mr. Prince comes off the elevator, andhe has a big ass grin on his face. Not wanting to mess up his great mood now, shequickly ducks into her office and sits down in her chair. All the whilethinking that he would not be this late. Something must have kept him from contacting me sooner.

After a few more minutes he goes into his office and screams, "Ms. Lucky. Myoffice!" She gets up and quickly goes to his office.

He then asks, "What are you waiting for? Go do the morning briefing Ms. V.P.!! Also one of your jobs in my absence. Come on now."

"Oh, my. I was waiting on you sir." Says Julissa. "I didn't know where you were. Plus, you didn't send me any information as to what to announce. You would haveusually sent me an email with the briefing subjects. New month, so I didn't have anything to share with everyone. You are never late."

"You are correct, and I wasn't late today either." He says "Also, since you're looking all crazy. I was in the bathroom." He explains. "Can a man have some timeto do his business without everyone panicking?"

"Oh, yes that definitely makes sense, Mr. Prince." Says Julissa. "For today can youplease go and do this briefing sir. I still don't know what the announcements are."

"Sure, Ms. Lucky. I will be right in. Please go and make sure everyone is in the conference room and ready." He says.

"Yes, sir, right away." She says.

"By the way, I'm guessing you didn't get the email I sent you last night about 11:30P.M. telling you that you would be doing the morning briefing today and to tell everyone to work on their specific jobs given to them last week." He says

"Wait what? I didn't receive an email, sir." Says Julissa.

"Well, I sent it last night, when I thought I would be late this morning due to a greatnight last night."

"Anyways that is beside the point. We need to get this issue out in only a few weeks and there's a lot more to add. Have you briefed Mr. Michaels on the thingshe needs to finish before all of his paperwork is done? Do me a favor and go andread that email and read it as I do this morning's very late briefing." Mr. Prince says as he goes to the conference room.

"Yes, sir, right away." She agrees.

Over the loudspeaker, "Everyone please report to the conference room." Julissaannounces.

Mr. Prince then comes into the conference room. He then says:

"Good Morning, everyone. Welcome in. I take it you all had a great weekend and are ready to go back to work this week and get this next issue out and on the pressby the weekend."

Everyone is yelling loud and clapping, saying, "Yes, boss. We are ready."

"Happy to hear that so that means we are all working on our parts to finish this intime for print, or possibly a little earlier. Briefing dismissed. Now, get to work!" Hesays.

He walks by Julissa's office then doubles back and says, "One major part of your jobnow is to always check your emails regularly. You never know when I will have tobe late even though today I wasn't."

"I actually did check my email Mr. Prince and there still was not an email fromyou." Says Julissa.

"Let me go and check. Just to double check." He says.

He walks back to his office and checks his sent emails, and he sees that he never sent the email. Feeling extra awkward. He then goes into Julissa's office and closesthe door, and apologizes from the bottom of his heart. "Sorry Ms. Lucky, but I actually did not send it." He says.

"Oh. It is okay, Mr. Prince. I just knew I never got an email. I wasn't going to makea big deal, but thank you for confirming."

As she is talking to him, her phone rings and she sees it is her mom. Thinking thatshe never calls her while at work, she lets him know she needs to take the call, andhe leaves.

"Hey, mom, to whom do I owe this honor of a phone call from you today?" SaysJulissa.

"Oh, nothing, boo bear. I just haven't talked to you in a while and I just wanted togive you a brief call to check on you." Mama Lucky says.

"I am fine, mom." She says.

"Oh, okay. That is great to hear, love. Well, I am going to let you do your work. Wecan talk a little later once you get off." She says.

"Okay, mom. I love you. Talk to you later. Bye" and they hang up.

She then walks back over to Mr. Prince's office and asks was he finished or wasthere anything else he needed to talk about?

"Oh, no, but since you are here. I will be having a longer lunch today." He says.

"Okay, no problem. I will definitely be checking my emails while you are out." Shesays.

"Good deal." He says, "That is just what I need you to do, and also make sure everything around here runs smoothly while I am gone. That most likely meansyou will need to take lunch once I return, or get something from the cafeteria delivered."

"Of course. No problem." She says "Also, one of our employees Jennifer, had anaccident last night and she will not be back for about a week until her arm heels."

Says Julissa.

"Oh, no. What kind of accident? Is she okay? Okay. Well, okay, just please makesure she is sent all the information she needs for her section. Is she able to do anything, or just on doctor's care at this time? He asks.

"Yes, I will make sure she gets her things to do at home this week. She just has asprain. I will explain later, but she is okay." Says Julissa.

He goes back to his office. Julissa gets comfortable and gets on her computer. Shelogs into this week's issue of the magazine to see how far everyone has gotten.

Trying to see who she needs to speed up a little. She sees about 5 employees thatare really behind and she announces for them to come to her office.

"Can I please have Darell, Paul, Tara, Kensy, and Lena. I need you all to come tomy office."

They all get up and head to her office as quickly as possible. She starts telling themall why they are in her office, and everyone says the same thing, "We are sorry and would get things up to date soon."

"Okay, I will be checking on you all by lunchtime, and if you are not at least half done then I am going to cut off your lunch from 45 mins to 20 because this is veryimportant especially with the spots you all are in for the beginning of the magazine. I am serious. Now, go and get to work."

"Yes, mam." Says the employees.

They all leave her office and go back to their desks. Julissa then calls Dennis into her office. She realizes he needs to sign the rest of hispaperwork, so he can go and do his photoshoot. The photographer is here today, and they need to get those proofs today.

He walks in and says "Will Mr. Prince be here too? I don't see him. You know whatI said." Says Dennis.

"I'm pretty sure he will be a little busy today so probably not. But we really needto get these things done today."

She hands him a stack of paperwork. "Here, sign these and I will confirm all signatures. Then I will need you to head to our studio for pictures." Says Julissa. "Oh, okay. Can I sit here?" As he looks at the chair next to him. "What is all this stuffanyway?" He says.

"If you skim through it you will see that it is just your bank information, so that you can get paid, and just some other information we need for your file to get in the system. Just read it. I will give you about 45 minutes to read and sign, "says Julissa "That should be plenty of time."

"Well this looks like a lot of reading. I don't read that fast. I'm not sure about all that, but I will try to do my best."

"Just take it to the conference room and fill it out, and bring it back once you are done. Chop, chop." Says Julissa as she motions for him to leave her office.

Julissa then calls downstairs to the studio and tells Percy Grahamer to let the photographer know that Mr. Michaels will be down in about an hour to take his pictures.

Percy says, "Okay, sure. Not a problem. I will let him know right away because he was getting a little antsy a few minutes ago. I did not have anything to say to him so I just asked him to please be patient, and I would have an update for him soon."

He says

"Great. So he was okay with that? Just give him my message please and thank you." Says Julissa.

"I will do just that Ms. Lucky" Says Percy.

"Appreciate it. Also, let me know what he says, especially if he is upset, but it's been a madhouse up here this morning. Just finally getting things on track." She says.

"Yes, ma'am. I sure will." He says.

Julissa does a few more things with her computer such as checking files, and making sure there aren't any new emails she needs to check and read. She also checked on the progress of those 5 employees and saw that they were moving pretty fast. "I guess my little talk with them really put some fire under them, or they really need that 45 minute lunch?" Either way she was happy. She then gets an alert of a new email. She checks it, but it is not Mr. Prince. It is just some random emails she can check later. She just had other pressing things to deal with at this time.

It is almost lunchtime and the phone rings. It is Mr. Prince. He tells Julissa that he will be leaving in about 20 minutes and will be returning back later due to some personal issues he has to deal with today.

She says, "Okay, no problem. I will hold it down here until you return."

"Now you are sounding like a V.P. Keep that up and you will do fine." He says and hangs up.

Julissa then starts surfing the net, and ends up on her social media. She watches a few videos for a bit, seriously cracking up.

She must have been on for quite some time because she then sees Mr. Prince heading out for lunch.

Once she saw him leave, she walked out to the floor and announces to the crew "Just because Mr. Prince is gone, that doesn't mean you all get to slack. You all need to get to work and help us finish this deadline."

Everyone then says, "Yes ma'am," and goes back to work. After about 2 hours Mr. Prince returns from his extra-long lunch. As he is walking into office he motions for Julissa to come in too. She then follows him and he says to close the door. She does what she is told.

He starts by saying, "I know you have only been at this position for a short time, but you follow directions very well, so what I have to say doesn't seem like itwill be a big problem for you."

"Okay, it feels like you are stalling, spill it, Mr. Prince." She says.

"I am going to have to send you to our office in California, first of all, to handlesome business over there." He says.

"Wow, California, Mr. Prince? I have never been to California." She says.

"Yes, Ms. V.P. There are some odds and ends I need you to cover over there, andseveral other spots before the week is over. Will that be a problem?" He asks. "Oh, no. Not a problem at all." Says Julissa.

"I need you to talk to the traveling and services department and get those flightsbooked by the end of today." He says.

"Okay. Right away, Mr. Prince." She says.

Julissa quickly goes up to HR and gets the information taken care of.

"You are now all set up. You have flights booked for the next 4 days. You will betraveling to California, New York, Virginia, & Texas. They will be daily stays.

Then as of Friday you will be heading back out here to Georgia unless you want tostay longer, but you will have to take care of those costs yourself." Says Othelia, the administrative assistant.

"Okay. That sounds great. Thank you." Says Julissa

It was getting late now, and Julissa needed to talk to Tim before she had to take these trips. She started to pack up her things to get ready to head home. It had been a verylong day.

As she's finishing up Mr. Prince stops by her office and gives her the information that she will need it for her business meeting and send her on her way. "I will see youonce you get back," he says. She walks out to her car and heads home.

It is around 6:30 P.M. She is sitting in some pretty bad traffic as she is on her way home. She tried to see why they were all still sitting in this hot heat for so long. Shethen finally gets a chance to see what the hold-up was and realized that there was an accident, and it looked pretty bad. Soon after that, she finally reached where the accident took place. She sees a Black Lincoln and a windshield completely shattered. Two kids were in the backseat crying uncontrollably. She could also see an officer trying to pry the right passenger door off. At first, he was not successful, but then he tried again and got it off. The other door was stuck too and there was glasseverywhere, but for some reason no one else was in the vehicle still but the children. As she continues to drive through what looked like the worst accident ever, she sees a lady's bloody body and then in the other direction a man's body also covered in blood. There was a lot of blood. It looked terrible. Not sure if they were still alive, but there was no movement, and didn't look very good. As she looked back she could see that they finally were able to get the girls out of the car. She breathes a sigh of relief for them babies. They were not her kids. She thought but she felt sorry for them. The mom and dad didn't look like they made it, and the ambulance was taking their own sweet time getting to the scene. She finally gets tothe front of the line and drives on to her suite.

She gets there quickly. She walks into her suite, after what seemed like a pretty long day, due to the long wait after work. The phone rings and it is her mom. She quickly asked, if she knew who the people in the accident were? She then says "Oh, yes, boo bear. They went to my church." She didn't tell her any names but justsaid, "It's a shame the parents were not wearing their seatbelts, and a car came out of nowhere and hit them from the side. Thank God, the car did not blow up! They hit them on the side with the gas tank. The mom and dad were instantly thrown from the car, but the girls had on their seatbelts and stayed intact."

She intervenes and asks her mom, "Why did you call? It was not about theaccident. So, how may I help you?"

"Well, I told you earlier I would call you later. Don't you remember that boo bear?"

She asks her

"Yes, I do, now. Mom, I have so much going on with this new V.P. position. I'mactually about to be gone for the rest of the week."

"Gone? Where, love?" She asks.

"Business meetings all over the U.S. Pretty much?" Says Julissa.

"Well to change the subject, I do need to talk to you, love. Can you come by the housewhen you get a chance? I know you are always working so much, but can you please take a little break for little old me?"

"Sure, Mom, anything for you. Is everything okay?" She asks.

"Sure, boo bear, I just want to talk to you about something that has been weighing onme for some time now." She says.

"Well it might have to wait until I get back into town because I have to go out oftown for work until Saturday." she says.

"Oh no that is too long but I guess I understand. You have a new job and all that jazz,"she says. "Okay, I will be there Saturday around lunch time. Maybe you can whip us up some lunch and we can have this talk." She says.

"Dang, boo bear, I have to wait till Saturday?" She asked.

"Yes," she tells her. "That is the only day I have off this week. I will have plenty of offtime this weekend."

"Oh no, I don't want to wait too long. But Saturday will be fine."

"Okay, so, will 11:30 be okay?" She asked her.

"Whip us up something? I just caught that. Oh no, I do not think I will miss moneybags. I think you could treat me for lunch or something. I don't feel like cooking." She says.

"Well, my bad, smarty pants. I will come by and pick you up by 11:30 and we can goto the melting pot, it is a very nice spot in downtown, Atlanta."

"Oh, yeah, I have heard ofit, I have also heard some good things, too." She says.

"Yes, it is a great place to eat." She say. "The service is exceptional and they love me there.Will 11:30 be okay, Mom? We know how you like to sit and watch those reruns on Saturday mornings."

"Not this time. I need you up and ready. I will do you one better.I will call you that morning to make sure that you are up and moving around."

She sighs, but she agrees and says, "I will see you then, boo bear."

"Great, mom. I can'twait." She tells her and they hang up.

She goes into the kitchen and grabs a glass of Stella Rose. She really needed a drink. "I cannot believe how everything went with Dennis. He was a complete jerk,and I just cannot stand the way he went about making me look like such a fool. I cannot believe he just walked past me like he didn't even know me. Oh well, now the ball is in my court. I am going to milk this new job. He will not know what hithim. Mr. Prince wants him to shine. Okay, I will make him shine." She thought. "Well, of course, once I get back into town. Anyways I need to get my mind off of this dude. Tim is a good guy and I honestly could see us together for a longtime." She thought.

Just as she started thinking about him he calls her. "Hey, Tim," she says.

"Hey, Julissa." He says, "I was calling you because I haven't heard from you. I waswondering if I did something wrong?"

"No, I have just been extra busy."

"I have had to deal with a new employee, and things have been more of a hassle than I thought they would be. In fact I actually need to go out of town for business the rest of the week starting tomorrow." She says.

"Oh, my now. Where do you have togo?" he asked.

"I have to go to Texas, New York, Virginia, and California. I will be backFriday." She says.

"Oh, okay. I understand. I guess I will see you once you get back then." he says.

"This new job also includes some extra bullshit. More money, more problems as most would say. I never had to worry about these things before. I now have deadlines, and pictures with these clients that have to be scheduled, plus paperwork that is to be to the ceiling." She says.

"Sorry to hear that, babe. So, wouldyou like me to come over, and help you relax?" He asked.

"No, actually, I am doing okay. I just needed to win a little. I like when we talk because you help me feel better without even saying much. I guess you and I cameacross one another again for a reason." She tells him.

"That's what I have been telling you. You crazy woman! I came here to rekindle what we had in the past, and I have extended my stay to see just what that is. Our time together was nice, and I thought we were on the same page but since you there was no communication I started to wonder." He says.

"So, again, would you like me to come over and ease your stress just a little? You don't have to leave till tomorrow. What time is your flight? Would you need me to take you to the airport? Sure I would appreciate that. My flight is at 6:30 A.M." He pauses for a few secondsthen he starts making beeping sound like he is giving her a chance to say something. "Beep, beep, beep. Going once, going twice. Oh, well the offer is off the table now, you missed out, sweetie. No chance now!"

"Well, again, that is a no. Anyway, I am feeling you, too, but I just want to take it slow. Iwant to spend some time with you, but I have just been swamped these past few days." She tells him.

"How about you and I go to dinner Friday night. There is this niceCajun place I have been wanting to try since I got here, and I am sure you would love it." He asked.

"I actually have plans with my mom, this Saturday for lunch." She says, "And there is notelling what she wants to talk about. That woman can talk and eat." She finished as they both laughed.

"Yes, Friday will be great." She says.

"If you don't mind, can I call you tomorrow?" He asked.

"That would be great. Besides, things might even change, which I doubt, but one can wish, don't get me wrong, I love my mom, but sometimes our combo get alittle crazy!" She tells him.

"Julissa, really? How crazy could they really get?" He asked.

"Oh, you don't want toknow! Well, let's just say that is why I try not to take her too many places, becauseshe likes to cause a scene." She explained.

"Not, mama Lucky. I cannot see that, but oh well, I guess I will take your word for it."He says.

"Yes, you should, because I would rather not get into a full on conversationabout my mom's shenanigans." She says.

"All right, I will talk to you tomorrow. Good night." Tim says. She says good night and hangs up. Then she goes into the kitchen and pours another glass of wine. Thinking she needs to pack is kind of tiring.

Sitting back down on the couch, she puts her feet up on the coffee table and beginsto listen to the CD on her phone. Oh, my goodness, she had gotten it from a really good friend a while back. Patrick was a sweet and sexy guy whom she talked to many moons ago. She wonders whatever happened to him, and starts dreaming about the way he used to kiss her. It did not take her long to snap out of it since Alex decided to call at that very moment. Her brother and his timing. She thinks.

'Hey, Lisa," he says. "What are you doing up this late?"

She says, "First of all, why are you calling me thislate? You messed up my wet dream!"

"Yo, sis. That is just nasty!"

"You asked," she told him. "Plus, I am leaving tomorrow for work, but it was gettinggood and to answer your question. I am here minding my own damn business. Anyway, boy, what do you want?"

"Leaving? Where do you have to go?" He asked.

"Work stuff, bro. What's up?" She asked.

"Boy? Sis, I am seriously no boy, but since youall in your feelings and stuff I will let that one go, this time! There is not going to be any more boy comments got it?"

"Okay, well I was letting you know that I think I found the girl of my dreams." He says.

"You mean to tell me you are calling me to talk about another one of your littlecrushes, bro?" Oh my gosh, I can't believe this. I could be doing something better with my time right now! Dreaming! She thought.

"No, sir. She is the real deal."

"Okay, what's her name?" She asked.

"Tanae," he says.

She asked, "Tanae, who? Because that name sounds so familiar."

"Tanae James. She stays here a couple of blocks from your old apartment. We met at the grocery store about 2 months ago, and we hit it off. We have been seeing each other ever since. She is beautiful. Kind of thick, long hair, and dark brown eyes. She has her own place. I'm crazy about her already."

"Does she have any kids?" She asked.

"Yes, she has two twin girls. They are so sweet and cute. We can be and they are like me too." He says.

"Dang, bro, you must really like her 'cuz you don't date anyone who has kids already." She says.

"Yes, she is amazing! We talk every day. I have been over to her house a few times. She has cooked for me. She is a great cook. I've cooked for her and her girls too. Countless times we have gone to the park together."

"Have you slept with her?" Julissa asked.

"No, sis, we have just been enjoying our time together. This one is different. I don't just want sex, she really makes me smile, and we have a lot of fun together besides all that. Well, I just wanted you to know about her and just how much joy she brings to me. Oh yeah, I wanted her to meet the family, so you think Mom would make dinner one day, maybe next week?"

"Good luck with that, boo boo. We are going to eat lunch out on Sunday because she didn't want to cook. I can bring it up and ask her to give you a call though? She says.

"I would really appreciate that, sis. Thanks." He says.

"No problem, bro. You know I would do anything for you. You're my little brother and I love you even though you really get on my nerves most of the time." She says.

"Love you too, sis." He says.

"Well, happy and in love, I need to get off this phone. Seems like we have been on here for a while. I need to go pack and shower so I can get some sleep. Got an early flight in the morning. I'm happy for you if this is as real as you say it is. You need to settle down with a good woman and stop messing with all these hoes out here just looking for someone to take care of them. Sounds like she is going to be a keeper. I really want to meet her now, but for now, good night." She says.

He says, "Good night, sis. Sweet dreams." and hangs up.

She then goes into the bedroom and begins to pack her clothes. She finishes up with her packing and then decides to go and take a bath. She finishes up her wine and goes to get another glass and runs a hot bath. She lets the water run for a little while, because she'll be soaking when she gets in.

She walks in the bathroom after a few minutes more have gone by, and takes off her clothes and slowly sits down in the tub. The water slowly covers her body and it feels so good! She can see the steam coming off her naked body like a sex scene in a movie, except there is no sex involved here.

She thought. Damn I wish it was I haven't been touched in so long that I wouldn't know where to start. She just starts thinking about Tim, and how Friday night he can fulfill those needs of hers.

She can see him in this tub with her. Of course, it would be full of fresh rose petals.She loves the smell of roses and the petals make her skin so soft. He would grab a rose petal and slowly slide it across her shoulders and down to her breasts.

She would lean back and just let him rub it all over her body. Tickling her with every touch. He was always such a romantic. She truly missed that. She thought. He wouldthen grab her and hold her tight as a kiss and caress each other. Getting even more into her thoughts, she starts to feel something nice between her legs, as she slowly touches herself. As if it was Tim's fingers.

She quickly begins overthinking and soon is in a full on stroke with her fingers and enjoying every single bit of it as she's pushing in and out of her vagina. It goes on a little while longer. As she is coming to her climax, she begins to play with her clitoris so strongly that she falls back into the water and lets out a huge moan. This is unlike any orgasm she had ever felt before. She just sat there and thought, damn! I could have had him here forreal, but my ass trying to protect my heart, decided I would decline his offer. It's way too soon, but damn if he made me feel anything likeI just felt, it would have been well worth it!

Oh, well, no need to worry about it now.He is probably in bed asleep. I am sure he is not even worried about me right now. She thought

She jumps out of her crazy day dreaming and starts to focus again. Her mind is clear now and she thinks, let me get out of this stuff. She gets out of the tub, and dries off and wraps up in her towel. She goes and finds a night shirt, and throws iton and starts towards her warm bed and watches a little TV until she falls asleep.

Chapter 3

Work Stuff

The alarm plays. Julissa wakes up and quickly turns it off. She looks at the time. It is 4:30 in the morning. She wipes the crust from her eyes, and goes and turns onthe coffee maker. She then calls Tim to make sure he is awake.

"Hey," he answers the phone. "Good morning, beautiful. See, you could have been waking up to me instead of calling." He says.

"Oh my, it's too early for this. You cancome over as soon as you are ready. I just need to jump in the shower real quick."She says.

"Oh, well, is that an invitation? Yes." He says.

"Wow, no. I'm just saying. The door is open." she says.

"See you soon." He says.

Julissa goes and jumps in the shower. Just as she is getting out, Tim shows up. Hecomes on inside as he was told to do, goes to the kitchen, and pours himself a cup of coffee. He asks Julissa, "Would she likesome?"

She says "Sure, but then we need to get on out of here and to the airport."

"Okay, no problem. You will not be late. I will make sure you are there and haveplenty of time. The airport is not very far away. By the way, what about your friend Destiny?" He asked.

"Oh, shit! I forgot all about her coming today. I will have to call her. Damn! I hatethat I am going to miss her. Maybe she will be staying a little while. Hopefully Ican see her once I get back." Says Julissa.

"Yes. Hopefully. That would be great, if she could stay awhile." Says Tim.

"Oh, well, I guess I will find out later, but for now, we need to go." Julissa goes to the bathroom and grabs her suitcase. Gives it to Tim and grabs her jacket and a bag. Tim leaves out the door, and Julissa follows him to his car, when they get in, they drive on to the airport.

They get to the airport, and Tim gets out and opensJulissa's door. Grabs her suitcase out of the trunk and gives it to her. Hugs her tight, and says he will give her a call later on or he can call heronce she's free.

She says that sounds great and walks on inside. Once Tim leaves, Julissa gets in the small line and soon is in front. She puts in her information for her ticket, and then prints it out. She now goes to her seat to waitfor the plane to board. While she is sitting there, Destiny calls and asks, if shewill be there to pick her up at 12:00!?

"No, girl. I forgot to call you last night. Myjob is sending me out of town until Friday." she says.

"Damn, Lisa. It's a good thing I will be here for 2 weeks. I will still get to see you once you get back right? Do you mind if I crash at your place, while you're away?"She asked.

"Of course, I will leave word for you at the counter. They will give you a key to myspot. I will send you all the information you need." She says.

"Okay, that sounds likea plan." Says Destiny. "I will see you once I get home. Love you, boo."

"Can't wait to see you." Says Julissa. Over the speakers, Julissa could hear they were boarding the plane. She tells Destiny, and they get off of the line.

Julissa gets up and gets in line. She is so ready to get these trips over with and getback home. She hears her name over the loudspeaker telling her to come to the desk. She quickly gets up and goes there.

Once she is there, the attendant says there is a problem with the flight and she will have to take the next flight out, because they are overbooked and there's no place on the plane.

She then gets upset and says, "Well, this is for business. I have to get on this flight." Just in time, a gentleman, who accidentally heard their conversation said that he would switch with her. All he has is that she and him get coffee one day while we are there, and he would be okay with the change.

"Oh, no, I couldn't let you do that, sir. I am sure you booked your flight way beforeme." Says Julissa.

"It's no problem at all, missy. We were just on a little vacation. I really don't have to be back until tomorrow."

"Ma'am, she can take my flight now and I will take the next one. She is on a businesstrip and I would do just fine. What time does the next flight leave?" He asked.

"8:30 A.M." Says the attendant.

"Oh, okay. That is okay. I will be getting on that one, if that is okay with you, littlelady?" Says the man, looking at Julissa.

"Yes, thank you so much, because I have meetings that I will have to be in around 8:00 A.M. and if you're serious about coffee, just letting you know that I do have a boyfriend."

"Yes, I was serious, but not in a I-want-you kind of way. I am happily married to mylovely wife. Tell her Lucinda." Says Jacob, the man who exchanged his ticket with Julissa.

"Okay, well then it's settled you and I will be sitting on this flight and Jacob will becoming in later. I really need to get home, but he will love the peace and quiet while I'm away. He really is being a good sport about this, but when we overheardthat you needed to be on the first flight we figured we could help you out." Says Lucinda.

"Oh, wow. Hi, miss Lucinda," says Julissa.

"Hi, sweetie. As I said, we were listening and overheard and I suggested toJacob that he should give you his ticket and catch the next flight himself. He didn't want to, at first, but I convinced him." Says Miss Lucinda.

"All right, everyone. We will make an exception because it was our fault this time, but next time we will have to let her take her own flight." Says the attendant.

"I totally understand. I just really need to get to California today." Says Julissa, "I hope this does not happen with my other flights for the week. I actually have three other destinations before Friday."

"I'm sure they will be fine, but if you want, I can definitely check them for you," says the attendant.

"Can you? I sure would appreciate it if you could, because I am in business meetings all week that I cannot be absent for."

"Actually, I'm checking as we speak," She says as she types information into the computer, "for your name." Once she sees all flights that have been booked, she nods to her. "It looks good! The rest are all set. You have three others, correct?"

"Yes, ma'am." Julissa confirms.

"No issues with any other flight as of now. You might want to check back in themorning at least two hours prior to your flight, but honestly it is showing that everything is okay right now." Says the attendant.

"Okay, thank you so much for checking." Julissa grabs her new ticket, thanks her again, and goes back to her seat to wait for her plane to board. She is sitting for a while then she hears over this loudspeaker someone calling for her section to start boarding. She quickly jumps up and gets in line. They wait for a few more people to join the line then they startgoing down the hall to the plane.

"Oh my, this is great. We're going to leave in time for my meeting." Said Julissa. She saw Mrs. Cinder walking with the crowd just behind her and heard her say, "Well that is wonderful.I'm so happy that we could help you out."

"Oh, yes. Me too, Miss Lucinda. Your husband was so sweet for doing that for me. In fact I will take you both out for coffee as soon as he gets in. My meeting should be well over by then the time helands."

"Anyways, well, he hesitated a bit but I knew he would want to do something to helpyou out." Says Miss Lucinda. They finally make it to the plane. Everyone gets on and as soon as they do, comes a new set of seat fillers. They all get to their seats and put up their bags then the last set of people come to claim a seat, and just as they are about to close the doors to the plane here comes Jacob.

Mrs. Cinder was so surprised. She started smiling the biggest smile Julissa had seen in the short time she had known the lady.She was so happy. She grabbed him and squeezed him as if she hadn't seen him allyear. It was absolutely amazing. The whole plane started clapping and then Mr. Jacob sat down next to her and me. The attendant then comes over the intercom and begins preparations for takeoff. She says her pitch and explains all the other thingsand then the captain comes on and says everyone prepare for his takeoff.

Just as they begin to leave Julissa's phone rings. She looks at it and it is Dennis. She didn't want to answer but thought it might be about work so she did.

He says, "Hey. Have you left, yet? I was trying to see you before you left."

"Why Dennis? I don't want to see you. You and I have nothing to discuss."

"Well, I just want one more night with you, Julissa. After that if you want to never speak to me again,I will respect your wishes and just make this purely professional but if you like meagain you have to get rid of your so-called boyfriend." Says Dennis.

"Ma'am, we are about to take off! Can you hang up and put your phone in airplane mode please. I know you just heard the captain say we were about to take off."

28

"Yes, ma'am. Right away." She says to the flight attendant, and then back on her call, "Dennis I have to go!" She says.

"Well, just tell me yes or no before you hang up." Dennis suggests.

"I don't know. Can't say right now. I have to think about it." Says Julissa.

"Ma'am you have to get off that phone." The attendant said in a bit of anger.

"Okay, no problem. Bye, Dennis." she says and hangs up. The plane begins to move andthey are headed for the runway straight to turn around and head to California.

They then take off, and it is not too long before Julissa is fast asleep against the window. She missed the snacks and everything. About 2 hours into the flight, Julissa wakes up and wipes her face because she can feel slobber all down her cheek. She grabs a wipe out of her bag that she brought with her and then gets up to go to the restroom, just as she gets up to walk towards the back of the plane to the restroom the plane shifts slightly to the right and kind of jumped a little, it must have been a little turbulence.

She thought it must be, but it still almost scared the pee right out of her, but she still went on to the restroom. She hadto go now more than before. She quickly went on to the door, but it was occupied. She waited a few minutes, and the door unlocked and she went in and closed and locked it. She sat down on the toilet and did her business. Gets up and washed her hands, drove them and got back to her seat in a hurry. As soon as she sits back down in her seat more of turbulence hits the plane and shakes the whole plane.

The captain again comes on the intercom and tells everyone everything is okay, and the plane will be preparing for landing soon. They got a bit more turbulence and then you could hear the wheels going down and could tell we are slowing up a bit while stillin the air.

The captain says in about 20 minutes they will be landing. So, she starts to look outthe window and once again she starts a day dream about Dennis and what he reallywants from her. She's thinking so hard that she falls back asleep for a few minutes and sees Dennis in her dreams. He is laying on the bed and says, "Come sit down Julissa. I won't bite, well not unless you want me to."

She says "No, Dennis! What are you doing here? We can't do this! Then grabs herand pulls her close to him. She tries to support herself out of his grasp but he is too strong. He then kisses her on her neck and she moans in pleasure. He kisses her again this time on the other side of her neck and again she moans. "Stop, Dennis. I have a boyfriend and you know that already." Says Julissa.

"Where he is now?" He mentions, "I don't see him anywhere, but you are certainly enjoying me right now."

Dennis then grabs one of Julissa's fingers and puts it in his mouth and starts to suckon it like he is sucking a lollipop. Julissa instantly feels something wet in her panties and she knows what that means, but she hesitates because of her boyfriend,but he is so persistent that Julissa easily gives in. He starts kissing her breast. Also sucking and licking her nipples until they are almost pulsating from the pain and pleasure she is currently experiencing. She moans in so much pleasure that at that moment, when Dennis goes down to her belly button and licks it, Julissa starts shaking. He then goes down to her vagina where she was already dripping from thesatisfaction she was feeling. He puts his finger inside her and then takes it back outto see how wet she was, and his fingers were full of her juices. He pushes it back inside this time with a little more force as she grabs his shoulders for stability. He pushes it faster and faster, until she screams with pleasure and that she is cuming.

As he is pulling out his finger she grabs his dick and says, "Put it in me. I want to feel it all. Since you want to do this, I want it all inside me, and don't hold back. Fuck me Dennis! Fuck me hard!"

Dennis slowly puts his manhood inside her vagina and begins slow strokes. At first he started moving slowly, and then faster and tighter her grip got on his shoulders. He turns her over and he puts his dick inside her vagina again as he pushes in doggy-style. She sent small thrusts back at him, and he pushed faster and harder until she climaxed.

They both just laid there once they were done. She quickly says, "You need to go!"

"What, no cuddles?" Dennis asks.

"Oh, no!" Says Julissa.

"Okay. Well, then, I'll leave." He says.

"Good, and this can never happen again." Says Julissa. "I can't control myself around you and I know better. This is just unreal. Stop toying with my emotions. You know how my feelings were for you. Just leave me alone. I got so caught up in all of this emotion that I forgot I hate you. I'm sorry but the way you disrespect me, I just can't go back there again. Just go!"

She pushes Dennis towards the door, opens it, and slams it shut.

"Wake up, we are here." Says Miss Lucinda as she nudges her.

"Oh, okay. I'm up." She says as she wipes her face and fully wakes up.

"Now, don't forget your bag, sweetie. It's on the floor." Miss Lucinda also says, "Oh, I won't. Thanks for reminding me." Says Julissa.

"No problem at all." Says Lucy.

They all begin to get off the plane and head for the baggage claim to get their bags and go on to their particular destinations. She gets to baggage claim after a while and walking halfway through the airport. Everyone waits for their plane to come up.

People are getting antsy waiting. Finally, the light comes on, a bell rings, and their luggage starts coming out on the rack. First, nobody's luggage came out but Lucinda's bag showed up and Mr. Jacob grabbed it. A few minutes later Mr. Jacob's bag comes through. We waited and waited but Julissa's bag never came through.

She goes to the counter to ask what the problem is and why her bags did not arrive like everyone else's.

"Well, ma'am you were supposed to pick your bags up here, but for some reason they were put on the flight you were set up on and not the flight you came in on." Says the lady at the counter.

"Okay, so when will I receive my luggage?" Asked Julissa.

"This afternoon, ma'am." She says.

"I am not that old lady. My name is Miss Lucky. Thank you. I will be back later this afternoon to retrieve my bags."

"Okay, Ms. Lucky, that will be fine. I will make a note of it." She says.

"Is everything okay, sweetie?" Asked Mr. Jacob.

"It's not at the moment, but hopefully this afternoon it will be. They put myluggage on the wrong plane." She says.

"Oh, no. Sorry about that. Okay, well since you got it all figured out, we are going togo home. How about we meet up later for that coffee?" He asks.

"Sure thing. If it's no problem for you two. See you then."

She grabs an Uber, and heads on to the office where the meeting is being held at 1459 Franklin Street. *One Take* a magazine from California. She arrives at the office, and goes and checks in with the receptionist. She says, "Good morning, Miss Lucky, we have been expecting you. Everyone is meeting in the conference room.Three doors down and to the right."

"Thank you so much." Julissa as she starts down the hall to the conference room. As she enters the room there are about seven other people inside, waiting for her arrival. She says hello to all the members, and then the president welcomes her.

His name is George Tyler. He asked her to introduce herself. She then does as she is toldand then sits down. They talk about new changes happening to the magazine. The president gives them all the information, and soon dismisses them all for lunch, and asks her to wait behind because he needs to have a word with her.

Everyone walks out of the room, and then the president closes the door, and says, "Congratulations on your position and your promotion! Mr. Prince mentioned that you are the new VP of our branch in Georgia."

"Thank you." She says.

"Oh, we will provide your hotel and other expenses while you are here. We justneed to get your personal information so we can make sure it is all prepared foryour state once it comes up."

"Well, we are done here. I just wanted to give you those extra details about your newpromotion. I'm going to have you head on over to our HR department. And get youset up in our system for your training." He says.

"Not a problem. I would do that right away." Says Julissa. She then goes on to HR andgives the info she needs to give.

"You're welcome." He says once she is done with everything and thanks him for the co-operation on the matter.

"Well, due to your promotion, you will be coming up here in a few weeks for training. It will last about a week, and once it's done, you will receive a check for

$2,000. Just a welcome bonus for all that you do, or will do for this company."

"Oh my, really? So when is this training?" Julissa asked.

"It will be from July 18th through July 24th. Says Mr. Tyler.

"Oh, okay. Those dayswill be no problem. I will be I'll be back here."

She finishes up in the office and then decides to go back to the airport because her suitcase should be there by now. Thinking about how she still received no call from the airport. She books an Uber and waits for it to arrive, as it said it was 10 minutes away, and while she is waiting, she runs into Jacob and Lucy sitting at a nearby cafe. She then goes over there, sitswith them, and orders a coffee. They talk for a bit. She checks the app and sees that her Uber was due to arrive in 5 minutes. So, she quickly says that it was nice to meetthem, but she needed to go to get her bags.

A few minutes later her Uber arrives. With the license plate mab14z6. His name was Charlie. He got out and opened the door for her, and closed it once she got into the car and verified where she wasgoing, and started the ride. As they were on their way, she received a phone call. It was the airport. They told her that her bags just arrived and they would be there waiting for her atthe check-in. She thanked them in return and told them that she was on her way and would be there soon.

They arrived at the airport. She goes in and gets her bags and then confirms her ticketfor her flight. Goes to her section and sits down. There was no way she was checking any more bags. She thought as she is sat, she decides to go and grab a drink Better yet a shot. A few hourswent by, and it was time to board. It was now about 1:30 P.M. Time to go to mynext destination. She thinks.

She then gets on her flight, and heads to New York. The plane lands in New York, andthen she goes to her hotel for the night. Gets into the shower and just lets the waterfall down over her face. She gets out of the shower. She then dries off, and puts on a t-shirt and panties. She finally gets into the bed.

It is early but she is so tired that she easily falls asleep.

Chapter 4

Work stuff (New York)

Julissa woke up from a crazy dream. Look at the clock, and it is 2:00 A.M. She gets up and go to the kitchen to grab a bottle of water. She then go and turn the TV on to see what's on, but unfortunately there was nothing. All she could hear was noise, in sirens from the outside.

And all she could think at that moment was that New York was a madhouse! It was her firsttime in the Big Apple and the stories were true. She sat for a while on the couch untilshe fell back asleep. After sleeping for a couple more hours, she hears her alarm go off. She quickly jumps up and goes on to the restroom. She pulls back the shower curtain and turns on the water.

She then feels the water and realizes that it's justright. She takes off her clothes and gets in the shower directly under the water, and lets it fall over her face and head. It felt so good the water was so hot and satisfying, she thought. While she is in the shower all she can hear are sirens. It is like 6:30 A.M. and this place has a lot going on, she thought. She gets out of the shower and finds something to put on.

She decides on a dress for the day. I mean damn I am in the big apple. Go big or go home, right. She thinks to herself. Anyways, she decided on a pretty pink one. It was fitting just right with a V-neck, and a slit of the right thigh. It was extra sexy. She added a gold necklace, bracelet, and a watch. Found some black heels to finish off the outfit.

She books an Uber. And in the meantime, starts to make coffee as she waits for her Uber to arrive. After afew minutes, her coffee is ready and she quickly pours it into a coffee cup, adds creamand sugar and gives it a quick stir before taking a sip. Oh my gosh, that's hot! She thought, as she drank it a little too fast. It burned her tongue and she can feel a little blister in her mouth. She grabbed a piece of ice out of the freezer, and began to suck on itfor a while.

Before long, her Uber app is dinging. She takes a quick look at her phone and it says her Uber is 3 minutes away. She grabs her bag, some things for her meeting, a light jacket, and then she leaves out of her hotel room.

While getting on the elevator, her cell rings. She sees it is Tim, so she answers andsays, "Hey, you, good morning. I can't talk long, but you got a few minutes till my Uber shows up."

Tim says, "Hey, babe, how are you? It has been a few days. How did your first meeting go, yesterday?"

"I am good, babe. I was just extra tired. It was a pretty quick day, then I back on my next flight to New York. I am still in New York right now. I will be leaving for Texas this afternoon after these meetings. I have two meetings today. Well, one is at 8:00 A.M.and the other is at 11:00 A.M. Then I will probably eat some lunch, get a quick few hours of sightseeing before my flight to Texas at 5:00 P.M. Oh, no at 5:40 P.M. sorry about that."

"Oh, okay. I was just checking on you 'cuz I hadn't heard from you. Just making sureyou got in okay, and are enjoying yourself. Hopefully not too much withoutme there."

"No," she says, "it's all been professional. Haven't done anything besides work, with these meetings and these people. My Uber just arrived. I need to go. I will call youbefore I get on my flight this afternoon."

"All right, babe." Tim says, "I miss you. Talk to you soon."

"Okay, babe," she says as she hangs up the phone. She then gets into her Uber and he confirms the destination. She agrees and he drives off and on to the office buildingfor the meetings. In about 10 minutes, she gets to the address, she tells him thank you, and then gets out of the car to goes inside. On her way up, she goes to the Uber app and sends him a tip for being such a good driver and being so sweet.

She gets to the receptionist's desk and lets them know why she is here and they onceagain send her to the conference room, but she is kind of early so she just sits downwith the few others and just makes small talk before everyone else arrives. Once everyone finally comes inside they get started with the meeting. This time they are discussing the financials of *One Take* of New York.

Mr. Winstonjust explained that the company will be picking up extra hours this month, and gave everyone a sign-up sheet to sign, if they wanted to work some of those extra hours. A few people signed up, and then Mr. Mark says meeting adjourned.

And everyone gets on up and leaves out and back to their jobs. She stops Mr. Markas he was walking out of the door, and asks him if this applies to all employees?

He says, "You are a VP, correct?"

She says, "Yes."

He says, "Well that is a no, then. You are asalary employee. Your money will not change unless you get a raise."

She says, "Okay, yeah that makes sense."

"Yes, ma'am." He says.

"Well," she said, "I'm going to go and experience all of the Big Apple and thenI will be leaving to my next destination."

"Oh, okay, Miss Lucky. It was nice to meet you and speak a little with you."

"It was my pleasure. Goodbye, gonna go and do a little sightseeing before my flight." She then goes to see a few things that she's always wanted to see if she ever came to NYC. So, she went and saw the Statue of Liberty. It was absolutely gorgeous. She was so big and beautiful, but so much better than she had heard about. Then a few hours before she had to get on to the airport, she had one more place she wanted to visit which was the Empire State Building! It was so high. She almost got dizzy going up to the top.

Of course, she couldn't leave here without going to Times Square and doing a little shopping. Then her last stop, before she was going to the airport was the radio City Music Hall. She was at each one of these places for a brief moment then it was off to the airport. Just so happened thatshe kept the driver all day, and he said he would show her the sites. It was a great end to her little stay in the Big Apple. She truly enjoyed herself and bought a few cute items to bring home with her.

He then takes her to the airport. It is now like 4:00 P.M. when they get to the airport and she gets out and gives him a $50 tip for waiting on her, and helping her see the sites, then said thank you and gets out and grabs her bags. He already has waiting for her. He was the sweetest. She then goes inside and directly to the security checkpoint TSA. She was able to bypass everyone else. It was great. This job has some amazing perks, she thought. She found the area she was already headed to,D25 for Houston. Boarding was about to begin in 30 minutes, while she was sitting to get ready for early boarding she decides to get a quick drink.

She orders a vodka and pineapple in some garlic parmesan wings. It was just a little something after the sightseeing. New York hadso much more to see, but she will definitely be coming back to visit for at least a few days. But in the meantime, she will remember what she already saw. After a little while longer, they called her the speaker that we were boarding in 5 minutes. She finishes up her drink and wings and heads back to her seat. Then decides to move closer because 5 minutes will go by pretty fast. They start lining up to board, priority first, which was her and about 15 other people. Then she goes on and gets on the plane after she scans her ticket.

Flight was about another hour and like 55 minutes.Soon the other passenger starts to get to their seats, and just a few minutes later, they have gone through the rules and regulations, and instructions and they are preparing for takeoff.

This time, Julissa quickly drifts off and after about an hour or so she wakes up and drinkssome water and sees that they are almost there. Again, she drifts off back to sleep, and then all of a sudden, she can hear the wheels dropping as they prepare for their landing in Houston, Texas. She starts getting her stuff together, and going out of airplane mode to set up her lift once she makes it into the airport. She had a good nap, but she was not most definitely ready for the bed. She goes online and books a ride then just waits till they land. She had her bag with her so she wasn't worried about having to go to baggage claim. Finally the plane lands at about 8:00 P.M. and they all rush off the plane.

She goes straight to the rideshare pickup, and her lift is just driving up. It was a Black Infinity. Very nice car. The driver does not even get out to grab her bags. He just opens the trunk and says to put her bags inthe back herself. She puts her bags in then gets into the car, and he verifies her name and destination and proceeds to the hotel to drop her off. It takes about 30 minutes to get to the hotel, and then again, he opens the trunk, and says, "You have reached your destination. Have a great night." She mentions that he will not be getting a tip, and he just drives off.

She goes inside and tells the concierge who she is and they give her the room key and tell her where to go. She quickly heads to the elevator, and goes up to her room. She gets there, goes inside, puts down her bags, and sits on the bed, then turns on the TV of course. Straight to the news channel, then starts flipping through the channels for something else like a hallmark movie. She finds one but she isn't sure what the name is, but it's a pretty good part so she just continues watching, and before she knows it is 10:20 P.M.

She then goes and jumps in the shower realizing she has to be up in about 8 hours. Her first meeting started at 9:00 A.M. tomorrow, she thought. She figured she would wake up about 6:00 A.M. Go get some breakfastand head to the meeting destination. She takes a nice hot shower, grabs some super comfortable pajamas, slides into the covers, and falls fast asleep.

Chapter 5

Work Stuff (Texas)

The alarm goes off and she just lays there for a little while longer. She eventually gets her lazy ass up, throws on her robe, grabs the room key, and heads downstairs to get some breakfast. There are all kinds of things to eat. She sees pancakes, eggs bacon, sausage, and even oatmeal and grits. All kinds of drinks include coffee, tea, orange juice, and apple juice. She grabs a plate and gets some pancakes, eggs, and bacon. She loves bacon. She thought, I don't usually eat much pork but today I wanted some bacon, and a cup of coffee. She gets her food and headsback up to her room.

Turns on the TV, and drinks a little bit of a coffee and for syrup on her pancakes, and grabs a slice of bacon. Yum, it tastes so good, she thought. She finishes up her food, and then goes to get into the shower. She takes a quick shower, grabs some clothes out of her suitcase, and lays them on the bed, as she puts on her makeup and does a little something with her hair. She decided on a natural look for her face today, and she put a few curls in her hair just to give it a little body. This texture is heat crazy, she thought. I am sure these curls are not going to stay long, but I'm going to try it anyway, she thought.

She finishes up her hair and puts on her clothes. She decides on a pink silk blouse in a pair of black slacks. She can hear herphone ringing, so she goes and answers it. It is Tim, he says, "Hey, babe, good morning How are you this morning? I didn't hear from you last night, so, I figured you were tiredafter your flight once again."

"Yes, I was extremely tired once I got into my room, babe." She tells him. "It was crazy. The driver was a total asshole. I got to the airport and after that I took alittle while to get to my room. Then I realized howlate it was. Took a quick shower, and got into bed. Babe, I am actually finishing upgetting ready for work, so, I can get on to this office for my 9:00 A.M. meeting. Howabout I call you once I'm done today?" I asked him.

"All right, babe. I'll be waiting for your call. I'm missing your sexy ass. Thinking about you a lot." Tim says.

"Oh, babe that is so sweet," I tell him.

She looks up at the clock on the microwave, and see it's 8:15 A.M., knowing she is not too far from the office from looking at the address on the GPS. She starts to relax a bit. It is only 20 minutes away. She thought.

"Houston is avery big town. I really need to go. Love you, and we'll talk later on today." Julissa says.

"Bye, babe." SaysTim in return as they both hang up.

After she gets off the phone with Tim, her phone rings again and is the guy on the line from downstairs saying that there is a car waiting for her. She sat there confused, because she knows that she didn't even set up a ride yet. So, she asked him to ask the person who they are. She waits as she hears him ask them who they are and they say, "It's Zetrick from one magazine. My boss sent me to pick her up."

"Oh, okay. I will be right down," I say to him. She hangs up and grabs her briefcase and her bag, and heads downstairs. Once she gets downstairs, she sees this tall, sexyman standing beside her favorite car. A black Audi. He is sexy. The car is sexy. He, then, opens the door, and says, "Hi, Miss. Lucky, I will be your driver while you are here, in Houston, visiting. Right now, I was told to take you to the office." He closes the door, and gets into the driver's seat.

"Well thanks for being so prompt. I was hoping to get in a little early, before the meeting starts."

"Oh, don't worry, Miss Lucky, I will make sure you are there and have plentyof time before the meeting. Plus, I think, Miss Jennings would like to speak with you before you all get started. Would you like to hear some music?" He asked.

"Sure, whatever you want to put on! I like all kinds of music." She says, "Let's hear 97.9, The Box, I've heard so much about it."

"Okay, there you go," as he turns it on andsome R&B song comes on with the nice beat. They start bobbing their heads to the music and head on to the office. A few minutes later, and a few miles down the roadthey run into some traffic.

Fortunately, Zetrick knows these streets like the back of his hand. He maneuveredall over the place, and before she knew it they were pulling up to *One Take*'s parking lot. The car stopped, he got out, opened the door for her, and helped her out. He grabbed her briefcase and took it inside for her.

She goes inside thinking this place is awesome. First of all, it is huge. Bigger thanany of the other office buildings I had seen. There were glass windows with goldchandeliers, and gold blinds. There was a big area set up for the employees. The ones who help make up the magazine every month. It was just so beautiful. She thought.

It was just about 9:00 A.M. Over the speaker someone came on, and told everyone waiting for the conference room to open to head there. It was down the hall, into the right. It was next to the break room. She walked inside, and sat downtowards the end of the big round table, but unfortunately the boss here had a betteridea.

"How about you come sit up here, close to me?" says Miss Jennings. "I need you to be in the leader's area. All of these people you see here and beside me are from all overthe world. This is what true leaders look like." She also says, "Take a good look at them, because, one day, you just might be in their same positions of power in this magazine. Miss Lucky."

"That sounds nice." Says Julissa.

"Well everyone, I think we can continue with our meeting. Just need everyone to introduce themselves, and then Eric will start with the morning announcements."

Eric gives the announcements and they all listen, and then Miss Jennings starts her partsand then goes over some things her team should know for the coming weeks. Soon, she dismisses everyone and tells everyone to get back to work. She then says, "Oh, Miss Lucky, can I have a word with you in my office please?"

They go to her office and quickly Miss Jennings asks her, "Why don't you move here and work as my VP? I have heard very good things about you and how hard of a worker you are, especially when it comes to your Georgia magazine. I would love to see what miracles you can work over here. Imean, don't get me wrong, we are good here, but it can always be better with theright person."

"Oh my, Miss Jennings. I am so intrigued that you would like that, but I love it in Georgia. My family and friends are there. I couldn't leave them."

"Well, just do me a favor and give it a littlemore thought, and here is my card, and once you decide either way give me a calland we can talk about it." Says Miss Jennings.

"Okay, I will do that." She says.

"Well, it was nice meeting you. Have a fantastic day. Ilook forward to your call."

"Sure, okay." So, she lives up as she walks out the door into the lobby to check on herride. As she comes out, Zetrich comes from around the corner and says, "Are you ready to leave, Miss Lucky? I am still your designated driver while you are here."

"Yes," she says. "I would like a ride back to my room then freshen up and change to doa little sightseeing before my flight this afternoon."

"Okay, ma'am, no problem." He says, "What time is your flight?"

"6:35 P.M. to Virginia."

"Well, it is only 11:00 A.M. so you have plenty of time. I'll have you there in a bit."

"Okay. Just take your time." Says Julissa. He turns on some music and they just groove a little. About 15 minutes later, they drive up to the hotel and he opens her door and she sits for a bit. She is finishing up a text so it takes a minute for her toget out. She then gets out and asks and says to Zetrick to wait outside. She should be in a few minutes.

"Okay, no problem," he says. "Okay, Miss Lucky. See you in a little while."

"Okay, sweetie, thank you so much."

"No problem. I'll be here." He says.

She walks to the elevator and presses her floor, and goes up to her room. Julissa quickly goes into her room and grabs some shorts and a baby white T-shirt. Quickly jumps into the shower for a quick once over and gets out and throws on the clothes she had out for her. She then grabs a bottle of water out of the fridge, and then walks over to the television and grabs her bag off of the chair.

She then heads out the door, and downstairs to the car and Zetrick waiting to takeher to do a little bit of sightseeing, before she has to leave. Looking at the clock in the car, Julissa could see that it was now about 11:20 A.M. Realizing the meeting was a pretty quick one, they drive off and go to a Cracker Barrel to get some lunch. He says that he has a small errand to run and he will be back in about 45 minutes.Zedrick drives off, and she goes inside and sits out of table. The waitress walks up and hands her the menu. She then says I'll give you a few minutes to look it over, and then I will be back.

Julissa says okay and thanks. A couple of minutes later the waitress comes back, and takes her order. She ordered a steak, and mashed potatoes with a side of veggies, and a sweet tea. She looks at her phone and realizes she has a few missedcalls. One from her mom and the other two from Tim. She first calls her mom, andgets her voicemail, so then she calls Tim back. He answers and says, "Hi, babe. I tried to call you earlier, because I had some good news I wanted to share with you."

"Okay," she says, "what is the good news?"

He then says, "I bought a house."

"Congratulations! That is amazing. How many bedrooms?"

"Three," Tim says.

"Why so many?" Asks Julissa.

"Well, you never know what could happen in the near future," says Tim.

"Oh, I have to go because my food is here. I will call you back later."

"Okay, babe. Loveyou."

"Love you, too." says Tim and hangs up.

The waitress puts down her plate, and gives her the drink and she begins to bowher head to pray and then begins to eat her food. Again her phone rings, and this time it is her mom.

"Oh, hi, Mom." She says.

"Hey, boo bear, how's work going? I know you are having fun. Where are you now?"

"Oh, Texas, mother. I will be flying to Virginia tonight. I have my last stop tomorrow. I will be meeting with the owner of the *One Take* magazine. The start of the magazine was in Virginia by Calvin Peterson. That man is a billionaire, Mom. Ireally should be reading up on him, so I know everything about him tomorrow. I heard he is very down to earth, and keeps you laughing."

"Oh, my boo bear. All I heard was that he is a billionaire," says Mama Lucky.

"Really, Mom? That is all you heard?" Asks Julissa.

"Yes. Honey, I heard that man is paid, is he single?"

"Why?" Ask Julissa. "I know you arenot trying to talk to him."

"Oh, no, boo bear. I was talking about you. What does he look like? Is he fine? A name like that would definitely a black man." Says Mama Lucky.

"Mom know that that man is probably old enough to be my daddy, plus, married with kids. I don't want him. Technically, he is my boss and can't be getting involved with the boss!"

"Anyway, girl. What are you doing? You were on my mind, so I decided to check onyou. Did they treat my baby okay? 'cuz if not, mama is going to get them!"

"Yes, Mom, everyone has been so sweet."

"They better be." Says Mama Lucky. "Well, boo bear, I have to go. I'll talk to youtomorrow after your meeting. Love you."

"Okay, Mama, love you. Bye."

Julissa hung up the phone, and finished eating her food. Then asked a waitress for the check. By now, she had been here almost an hour. She was done, and all ready to go. She lets her waitress know that she needs the check. A fewminutes later, the waitress brings the check to the table.

She says, "Thanks for dining with us today."

Julissa says, "Oh, no problem, a girl's gotta eat. Plus, the food was delicious." She then tells the waitress to wait a second, and goes into her purse and grabs a $10 bill and hands it to her.

"Thank you," she says.

She pays and steps outside to check for her ride. He is still not here. She goes backinside and calls him. He quickly answers, and apologizes for not being there and explains that he is less than 5 minutes away and just to wait inside. A few minutes later he shows up and comes inside to let her know and grabs the door andopens it. Julissa gets in and he closes the door, and goes to the dry receipt and they drive off. He then asked, "Where to, Miss Lucky?"

"I really don't know much about this place. How about you pick somewhere. I will follow your lead."

"Oh, okay, let's just go to the mall!"

"Sounds great. Shopping is always a great idea."

"All right, Miss Lucky. The mall it is." He says.

After sitting through a little traffic they soon pull up to the mall and Sugar Land.First Colony Mall. This time, Julissa tells him to come inside with her. They both get out and goinside.

Julissa walks in and has the biggest smile because she loves shopping. She stops at several stores. Couldn't walk past Victoria's Secret without checking out a few new bras and panties sets. Decided on two; a black see-through set and a purple set. Left there and then walked to Inter Foot Locker, because Julissa saw some sneakers thatshe really liked, and went inside to ask for the price. They were only $125 so she decidedto purchase them. They stopped at about four more shops. Some clothing, perfume, and electronic stores. Looking at the time, told Julissa that it was almost 4:30 P.M. and there might be traffic on the way back to the hotel, and then also on the way to the airport, so it would be a good idea to leave.

Okay, you know he plays better than I do, so whatever you think is best. We can go.They walk out of the mall, and back to the car. And ended up sitting in a bit of traffic on the way to the hotel once again, once they reached the hotel, she jumps out and goes on in and upstairs to her room to grab her things and put all the new items into her suitcase. She then grabs her bags and heads downstairs. Zetrick meets her, and grabs her bags and puts them in the trunk. They then get into the car and drive off to the airport. While sitting in traffic it starts to rain, and while Julissa is sitting there, she gets a call from Mr. Prince, her boss and he is telling her about her big meeting tomorrow with the owner of the magazine, and that if she makes a good impression it could mean a big promotion. Carefully, they talk for a little longer, and it is still raining. Traffic is still kind of bad but it seems to be starting to move a little. Julissa reassures him that she is aware of how important this meeting is and says she is about to be at theairport, and says goodbye and hangs up. About almost 45 minutes more they make it to the airport terminal C.

Zetrick parks in and gets out to get Julissa's bags and says have a safe flight. It wasnice meeting you. She gives him a $20 bill, and he says thank you and then leaves. Julissa walks on inside into the line to the counter to put her suitcases underthe plane. It took a little while, but finally got up to the front of the line and they took her bags and gave her the receipt tag. She walks on to her plane waiting area on 43A. A few minutes goes by and they start boarding the plane. They get to Virginia. While Julissa waits on her luggage to come through, she sets up a lyft rideto take her to her hotel.

She sees her bag. She grabs it and heads to ride-share pickups. As she's walking out her ride arrives, and she gets out, and grabs her bags and opens a jealous store and she gets into the car and then they drive onto the hotel. She'll listen gets out, and the driver gets her bag out of trunk and takes him inside for her to Julissa givesher a tip and goes on inside to get her keys to her room. Her room was on the bottom this time she goes to hcr room, and sits down on the sofa. It is 8:55 on the clock andshe is tired but hung hungry so she calls Uber eats, and orders something to eat from a seafood spot that they passed on the way in. She turns on the TV and while waiting for her food she grabs the t-shirt out of her bag, and jumps in the shower.

While in the shower she starts thinking about Tim.

She starts thinking about him in there with her. Thinking of him kissing her and touching her all over. He slides his hands down to her booty, and grips it right and tight and slowly picks her up. You sucks her breasts and how her body is so wet,she slips out of his grasp and she slides into the tub. He then turns her around and slides his manhood inside her. She moans and groans and he pushes in and out as she moans even more, Julissa can feel herself about to come. Thinking deeply that was fast, but it was feeling so good, she let it go. She grabs his shoulders as hestarts going and controllably and moans and absolute pleasure with each stroke.

Soon, there is a knock at the door. "Oh, shit," she says, "let me get out of here." She then quickly jumps out the shower and grabbed her towel and goes to the door.Gets her food and puts it on the table and goes back to the bathroom to finish up her shower. She finishes, then goes and eats her food, which to her surprise is still warm. She eats her delicious food and grabs a water from her fridge, and sits downon the bed turn on the TV and then looks out the window of her room to the outdoors, and again starts to daydream. Then she snaps out of it and decides to go to bed. Tomorrow is a very important day. She thinks as she closes her eyes and goes on to sleep.

Chapter 6

Tim's Big Night

Meanwhile in Atlanta, Tim is sitting on the couch and watching TV. He looks at the clock and sees that it is almost 8:30 P.M., his mind solely on Miss Julissa; he can't even sit still enough to seriously pay attention to what he is watching. He keeps thinking about how things would be, if he had a future with Julissa. He starts to daydream about their life, and how good it would be. He really cares about her, but he doesn't want to rock the boat with her by moving too fast. He started thinking back about the little situation with Julissa and that guy from a week ago. The argument looked pretty heated. She thought she played it off but nope. He saw a little bit before she saw him. If that was her man, he was very disrespectful. Walking up on him and another woman in the same hotel. Awkward, he thought, the phone then rings, while he is in such deep thought.

He sees it on the kitchen counter. He picks it up and it is Gerald, his boy from down the street. He tells him he is about to go out and have a future drink, and he gives him an invitation to go if he would like to go.

Tim says, "Sure, I could really use the night out with the guys. I have been dealing with my ex."

"Julissa?" Gerald says, "Tim, you know I told you I ran across her since I've been down here for my little visit."

"Yes, dude, but I thought that was over years ago. She gave your ass an ultimatum and you left anyway. She is not mad anymore? You know how that chick could really hold a grudge forever!" Gerald exclaims.

"Yes, I know she can be real, you know. What at times, but I feel like there could really be something with us this time." He says.

"Well, you do what you think is right, but just do me a favor and don't get all caught up in those old feelings you have for her, before you actually know the real deal?" Gerald says.

"Honestly, bro, I am already there, but I will be even more careful this time around. If there is one that is." Says Tim.

"Good to know, my friend." Says Gerald.

"Anyways, to change the subject, are you going out or what? We need to go on ahead and get there if we are."

"Yes, but I will meet you all there. I need to go and take a shower and freshen up a bit before I go." Tim explains.

"Sure, no problem, bro. I can smell your ass over here." Said Gerald.

About 45 minutes later, Tim leaves the hotel to go and meet his friends. He is wearing a black button down and some jeans. Looking all good and smelling good. He gets in his car and drives onto the spot. That is the name of the place they are meeting. Supposed to be a pretty nice place. He drives there and he gets to the door, and he is walking in and he sees his ex from way back looking fine as hell.

She speaks to him, and he almost loses his mind! He speaks back with his voice allraspy because she seriously surprised him. She touches his shoulder as she passes him, and his body tenses up!

He walks on in behind her, and as he comes in his boys are watching closely. Hewalks over to the burrow, where his friends are waiting, and they are all smiling with these big grants on their faces.

He quickly says, "Oh, no. That was just a coincidence. I saw her walking up when Iwas coming in so I let her go in first." Says Tim.

"Yeah, sure, isn't that your ex, Anaya?"

"Yes, it is, but nothing is going on. Notsaying I wouldn't enjoy a night with her but I am trying to see what happens withJulissa. I'm good. I'm sure, she got a nigga anyway." Tim says

"Well, how about you go and ask her. So, listening is just a thought. Y'all not backtogether yet, are you?" Gerald asked.

"Well, no, not really. Just kind of giving me the cold shoulder. But I don't want torock the boat before the boat is rocking if you know what I mean!"

"Oh, I know what you mean! Just think though. You could tap that tonight, and no one will ever know."

"Come on, man, stop being so scared. You know you want to havethat body on you tonight." He says.

"Well, I need a few drinks in me before all that."

He ordered a few shots of tequila. One for him and the other for Gerald. They getthem and take them quickly.

"Two more, please." Tim says.

They have a few more drinks, and Tim says, "Okay, I'm going to go talk to her."

"Julissa, who?" Gerald says sarcastically as Tim begins to walk towards her.

"Wait, man. She's coming to you instead. Hold on. Relax dude!"

"Really? Oh shit! Whyis she coming over here?" Ask Tim nervously.

"I don't know, dude. Just say hi." Says Gerald.

"Hi, again, Anaya. What are you drinking? Can I buy you another?"

"Yes, and oh, I'm drinking some Cîroc on the rock," she says.

"Wow, no mix?" He asked. "Isn't that a bit strong?"

"No. I have had a crazy week, and tonight I just want to free my mind and havesome fun!"

"What kind of fun did you have in mind?" John jumped in and asked her.

"I just wanted to drink, and then maybe have some adult after hour activities," as she turnsand looks at Tim.

Tim quickly swallows and has the biggest grin on his face and says, "I'm down forthat! You want to drink some more or are you ready to go now?"

"I want to dance a little more, and maybe have one more drink then we can go to myplace. How did that sound to you? Is that okay with you?" Anaya asks.

"Okay. That sounds like a good idea. I would need to go until, my boy, I am leaving."Tim says.

"That is fine. I will be ready in about an hour." She says.

Tim walks back to his friends and tells him what is about to go down! Geraldquickly says. "I told you she wanted you man!"

Tim says, "Damn, and she was so sure of herself. Man, I'm about to have sex with her tonight."

"Oh, damn, but what about…uh…?"

"Man, you can't even remember her name. How do you think you will get together?" Gerald asked.

"I don't know, man. I am so tipsy. I just want to get inside something tonight and sheis out of town right now. Plus, she might not be ready for me yet, quite like I know Aniya is, and has always been." Says Tim.

"You never know it might be a love connection?" Gerald says.

"Oh, no. I don't want to do all that. I just want to hit it and keep it a secret. I am nottrying to make anyone fall in love. Maybe, I should tell her no!" Tim says.

"What? No. Stupid man. She is literally handing you the nana, and you're going toturn her down? Man, if you don't want it, I'll take it." says David as he jumps in the conversation.

"She is so damn sexy in that dress. I just want to pull it off. Look at all those curves.Man, she is not supposed to look like that tonight. I need another drink. My buzz iswearing off," says Tim.

He then says to the bartender, "Can I have another drink? It will be my last one. I promise. I'm trying to hit it and forget it tonight!" He says.

It's been about 45 minutes since she came up to Tim, and she comes back and says,"Are you ready? I am ready to go now. I have had enough. I just want to be on top ofyou now!"

"Are you sure?" Tim asked, "'Cuz we can sit here a little bit longer. That's okay with you."

"What do you mean? Are you trying to say you don't want me?" She asked.

"Well, you have had a lot to drink. Are you sure you want to go through with this?" He asks her.

"Nigga, you were asking all the wrong questions. Why are you not asking me stufflike, am I wearing any panties? Which I am not, by the way." She says.

"Dude, if you don't go get that good good, I'm going to slap some sense into you."Says Gerald.

"Okay, okay, Anaya." He says, "I am ready to go. Let's go."

Tim and Anaya leave, and go back to her place. She didn't stay far. Tim left his carthere and went in hers. They get to her house and she opens the door and as she opens the door Tim grabs her ass. She makes some sexy moan, and they go on in. They start grabbing at their clothes and taking some of them off. He grabs her breasts, and dry humps her to see just how excited she is, which is very exciting. He grabs her dress and pulls it over her head and pushes her onto the couch and takes out his penis and puts it inside her vagina. He starts to push in and out, and she begins to moan. He says, "Damn, girl. How is your stuff this tight? Should feel sogood. I can't stop, I can't stop! I'm about to come. Can I come in your mouth? I am not going to nut you." says Tim.

"Yeah. When you get ready just take it out." She says.

"Damn, girl, why didn't you get a condom?" Says Tim.

"Well somebody wanted to getin this garden all fast and stuff! You didn't give me much time to grab one!" She says.

"Well, the next time, we going to use a condom," he says.

"You coming back?" Says Anaya.

"Oh, hell no! I am going to fuck you enough tonight that I won't need to get anymore. This is just for tonight. Remember that." Says Tim.

"Okay, whatever you say, but once you have this pussy you're going to want itagain and again. Please believe," she says.

"No, just tonight. It's good. This is true but it can't continue after tonight." Tim says.

She pushes him on the bed and gets on top of him, and begins to do all these tricks,and he is just taking it like he is a pro. This goes on for about another 10 minutes. She has some skills he thinks.

She screams I'm about to come and then she is coming! She gets off his dick. She grabs a hold of it so tight and begins to suck it. It is feeling so good right now. Shetakes it all and he is about to come, and she just keeps sucking. His body starts to get lent because she is making him so weak with everysuck. After a few seconds, he begins to come, and she sucks until it is all gone!

They fall back on the bed. She then says, "Nigga, I thought you were going to fuck a lot tonight?"

"Fuck that. I amtired. That took a lot out of me. Plus, I am drunk." Then he falls asleep hard.

A few hours later, Tim wakes up with the worst hangover, but he knows he must gohome. He wakes Anaya up and has her take him to his car. She gets up and grabs a row, and they walk out to her car. As they are on the way back to his car she keeps trying to touch him. He says to her, "Please, stop!"

"Why?" She asked.

"I do not want you to. That is why!" He says.

"Well, damn, I thought you enjoyed it, but I guess I was wrong." She says.

"No, it's not like that, but it can never happen again."

She can be seen driving him to his car. They get to his car and he gets out and getsinto his car and goes home. He gets to his suite, and goes on inside and goes directly to his bed and he is knocked out in a matter of seconds.

Chapter 7

Work Stuff (Virginia)

It is 6:00 A.M. Julissa wakes up thinking it is late, because she realizes that she forgot to set her alarm. She got on up and went to the fridge to grab a bottle of water. She then turns on the television just so she could listen to the news while shegets ready for her day. As she turns it on, it is a story about a mother getting shot at a nightclub or somewhere downtown. Julissa wasn't familiar with Virginia, but she continued to listen to a few of the stories until she hears that Carrie Hilson will be having a concert tonight at 8:00 P.M. She knows her plane was set for 8:15 P.M. butshe looked it up and bought a ticket anyway. She loved Miss Carrie, baby! She knew she was going to have to book another night, and so she also picked up the phone, and dial the front desk, and ask for another night. She wasn't leaving till the following day. She had to see Carrie, or she would regret it, she thought. Even set up backstage passes to meet her. She was so excited, as she jumped in the shower.

Singing turns me on. One of her favorite songs.

She finishes up in the shower, and goes to the kitchen and turns on the coffee pot. Hoping she can get a couple of coffee before she has to go. She started the coffee maker and then went to get dressed for her meeting today with the CEO of Virginia*One Take* magazine! It's 9:00 A.M. She puts on a little black dress and some heels, and a little bit of makeup, and heads to the kitchen area. It is 9:45 A.M. and she pours a cup of coffee. While drinking her coffee she goes online, and orders an Uber. It says20 minutes. She sets it up. She figures she would have just enough time to finish getting ready before her ride gets there. She sits down to drink her coffee and watches a little more TV. Her ride arrives exactly in 20 minutes. She verifies the address and they drive onto the headquarters1800 Kings Avenue is the address.

They get there. She hands him a $20 tip, and gets out and he drives off. She walkson into the building, and speaks to the receptionist and lets her know why she is there. The reception Rita says, "Oh, no problem. They are about to start. Go on in. The meeting is in the conference room." She then points down the hall.

Julissa nods that she understands, and walks on down the hall into the conferenceroom. Looking at the wall she sees the clock reads 10:45 A.M. She walks over to thetable to the right, and grabs her a donut, and one of the prepared coffee cups, and finds a seat at the conference table and then begins to eat.

A guy walks up to her, and introduces himself as Romero She nicely looks up andsays, "Hello, Romero, nice to meet you. I am Julissa. I am visiting your office from Georgia. How are you?"

"Oh, I am doing great," says Romero. "I woke up this morning feeling great, and readyto see about this promotion I just went up for."

"Oh, that is awesome! I hope you get it."

"Yes, me too," he says as he goes and grabs a donut and a bottled water, and walksback over and sits down next to her. "Is it okay, if I sit here." He asked.

Julissa motions that it is okay, and he sits down. "So, exactly what do you do herenow, if I may ask?" asks Julissa

"Oh, no problem, I work in the processing and editing department. I go overother employees work and confirm that it is ready for print." He says.

"That sounds like a pretty big job!" Says Julissa. "Yes, and no." says Romero. "Once you know what you are looking for it's pretty easy, but it takes time to learnit all."

"I totally understand. I'm the VP in Georgia and it took me 10 years to get that position."

"Wow!" Says Romero, "that's the job I am trying to get. I've only been here 6years, but, damn, 10 years is impressive! Congratulations! Well, hopefully you get it such, Julissa, yousound like you have earned it!"

"I'm not sure what all you know but it's a lot of work.Well, since I've started it's been kind of crazy, but I can handle pretty much anything that they have me to do, so they know, I am the right person for the job!"

The owner then walks inthe room and says good morning to everyone. We both say it back.

"Figures you two are the only one's this morning?"

"Oh, no, boss, there should be about five more. I'll go and see where they are."

"Well, thanks, Romero." as he quickly gets up and leaves the room. "That boy's going to makea great VP." Says Mr. Walters. "He knows all about *One Take*."

"Hello, Miss Lucky, I presume?" He asked.

"Yes, sir, I'm from the Georgia side." Says Julissa, "I know exactly who you are! Your name has been all over the business emails. You have been a great asset to *One Take*. You have signed over 20 people with us. Built some amazing contracts Camp, and I just want to shake your hand." And she shakes her hand.

She smiles, and says, "Well, you are pretty amazing yourself. I have read all about you, Mr. Walters."

Mr. Andrew Walters nods and says, "I see you have done your homework."

"But, of course, I didn't have to do much. I see your accomplishments through theportal. You have doubled what I have done here."

"But we are talking about you, young lady! Smart, talented and beautiful. May I ask you a question?" He asked.

"Sure, what is the question? She says.

"Are you single by any chance?" Heasked.

"Afraid I'm not, but why do you ask?" Says Julissa.

"Well, I figured a beautiful woman like yourself would be either a workaholic or with someone. You seem like the type that takes care of business!"

"Well, you got thatpart right. I definitely do take care of business! But aren't you?"

"What?" He asks.

"Married, or some shit. Excuse my French. I thought I heard you had a wife and kids."

"Wife? Kids? Where on earth did you hear that from? I have been married once in my life, but have no kids. I'm single and was hoping you were too." Says Mr. Walters.

"Oh, well, nope, I'm not. I have a boyfriend. We are very happy. I mean you are a fine ass brother that I would surely love to give a try but sorry it ain't happening. Are we done here? I mean why am I here today anyway?"

Just as they get through talking, Romero walks back into the conference room. "I found everyone but one. We'll just have to start without her."

"Why, yes, Romero. That sounds good. Let's get started."

"Good morning, everyone. I would like to introduce Julissa Lucky. She is a part of our Georgia office. She is the VP there. She has done some great things and I just wanted to introduce her to everyone here."

They then go over some things about the office there. They have the meeting. Just mainly talking about things that go on in the Virginia office, then Mr. Walters excuses everyone.

"Are we done here?" Says Julissa. "I really need to go."

"Well, yes. You are free to go. I need to go myself to get some things done before tonight."

"What's happening tonight? If I may ask?"

"Oh, I am going to the Cary Hills and concert tonight." He says.

"Oh, really? I am too. In fact I postpone my flight home so that I could be able to go." She says.

"Oh, so is that an invitation?" he asked.

"Well, I guess we could go together, but just as friends, colleagues or whatever you want to call it." She says. "I think it will be fun rather than us going alone. You seem pretty cool."

"Okay. Well we have like 6 hours until the show. You go and tie up whatever you need to, and send me your info and I'll pick you up around 7:00 P.M." He suggests.

"All right, that sounds good. See you then," says Julissa.

"Don't forget to send me your info." He says.

"Okay, okay, sending it now." She says.

"Got it!" He says.

"Well, I will be looking forward to seeing her, and by the way, I also have backstage passes." Says Julissa.

"Damn, girl, you got the deluxe pack, I see." He says.

"Yes, indeed. I love her. Her music, her style. Everything!" Says Julissa

"Okay, Miss Keri Hilson stalker, I get it. I get it. You love her!" He says.

"Oh, no homo or anything. She's just very talented and beautiful. I wish I was her. The money, the fame. I want it all!"

"All right, then. See you tonight. Concert starts at 8:00 P.M. So, I will pick you up by 7:00 just to make sure we get great parking." He says.

"Oh, about that. I also set up valet parking, so we can let them park for us and wecan be dropped off in front." She says

"Damn! Woman, you went all out. Okay see you in a bit. I got to go." Says Andrew.

"Okay." Says Julissa.

They both leave the office, and set out to finish up those loose ends before the concert later. Julissa decides to go back to her hotel, and take a good nap before getting ready. She was still tired from getting up so early this morning. She gets picked upby her Lyft and asks him to make a stop to grab a bite to eat. He drops her off a fewblocks down at the couple. She goes in and order the steak, and shrimp with baked potato, and a tea for her drink. About 20 minutes later, they bring her order out and she eats and while she's eating, she sets up another Lyft ride. It says that it's 10 minutes away. So, she finishes up her meal, and pays her tab then goes to the right waiting area in front towait for her ride.

A few minutes later, she looks at her phone, and it is now 3:15 P.M. Her Lyft showsup and she gets in and they proceed to her hotel. About 20 minutes later, they arrive, and she gets out and goes up to her hotel room. As soon as she walks through the door, she quickly starts to undress and slides into the bed.

Sleeping soundly for about an hour until her phone rings and it is Tim."Hey." She says in a low tone.

"Oh, my bad, were you sleeping, my love?"

"Yes." She says with that same low tone. "Okay, I'll call you back once I wake up." She says.

She sleeps for about another hour before her alarm wakes her up. It is now 5: 06 P.M. and she quickly gets into the shower. While in the shower, she is singing Carrie Hilson songs, and truly enjoying her shower. The water is hot, and steaming up theglass doors. As she is in the shower, she has flashbacks of Dennis and her sex in the shower. He washes her breasts, and slowly goes to her stomach, and then washes her back and shoulders, down her thighs and feet. Dennis slowly takes the washcloth and slides between her legs, and washes as the expression on her face changes into and all sensation as he drops the towel, and continues with his fingersas she moans and screams in pleasure. Just as she gets to the good part, her phone rings again and she jumps out of her fantasy, and out of the shower and grabs thephone just in time.

"Hey, baby, are you awake now? I have been really needing to talk to you." Says Tim.

"Oh, damn, babe. Well, what is so important you couldn't wait for me to call you back?" She asked.

"Well. Remember my homeboy that had that club?" he asked.

"Yes, what about him?" She says smartly.

"We are now partners. He asked me if I wanted to become a partner with the clubbecause he's always the way and I've been helping him."

"That is a great, babe." She says. "I know that makes you happy. So, you've been helpinghim since I left?" She asked.

"Yes, love. That's my boy. I had to."

"Again, that is great! More money. Sounds great." She says.

49

Looking at the clock, she realizes they have been talking for a little while and she needs to get dressed. She tells him she has to go because she is going to see CarrieHilson tonight.

"Carrie Hilson?" He asked.

"Yes, baby. I heard she was going to have a concert tonight so I postpone my flighttill tomorrow." She says all excited.

"Well, shit, when were you going to tell me?" Asked Tim, "you know I have to pick youup from the airport."

"When I called you back, but you called me instead. Anyways, I have to go. Mycoworker is picking me up at 7:00 P.M."

"Have fun, but not too much though. Hold on, who is this coworker?"

"Oh, the VP here in Virginia. He was going to the concert so we decided to gotogether."

"Well, damn, baby, now we just jumping in cars with strangers?"

"It's a coworker, babe."

"He's a nice guy. I figured it would be okay."

"You figured. Well, I don't want you going with him. It's dangerous Lisa."

"You don't want me going withhim? Well, since when did you become my daddy? I understand that you were worried about me, but I will be extra careful."

"Yes. I would prefer you not go with him, with this man whom you onlyhave known for a few days." says Tim.

"Well that is better! Even though I'm still going. Again I will be extra careful. Hopeyou can understand, but I am pretty good with judging of character, and he seems like a good guy. End of discussion! Again I have to go. Love you, bye." As she hangsup. Her phone rings again, and it is Andrew saying he is leaving his apartmentand will be there in 45 minutes.

Julissa listens then goes and gets dressed. She grabs a strapless red top with a pair of blue jeans shorts, and some red heels. She figures it was going to be hot. Brushes her hair a little bit and puts on white makeup. Sat on the couch to wait for Andrew.After a little bit he gets there, and calls to say he is downstairs. Julissa grabs a small clutch and her key card and heads out the door, and so the elevator and downstairs. As she gets off the elevator, Andrew is there, waiting for her. He grabs her arm and walks her out, into the car. No need for all that as she moves her arm away from him. "This is not a date!" Julissa says.

"Oh, I know. Just a man being a gentleman for a beautiful woman."

"Okay, then,I got a man. I ain't that kind of girl."

"I know, I know." He says genuinely.

They drive onto the concert. Once they arrive Julissa reminds him that she has a vallet setup. So they drive up and get out as the valet gets in and drives off. They walk inside. The concert hasn't started yet, so they get a drink, and go and find their seats. Their seats are actually close by. The concert then starts, and Carrie comes on stage looking amazing! She started singing and everyone started clapping and yelling her name, and she smiled and continued to sing. The concert was great! About 2 hours, and six or seven songs later the concert ends and Julissa gets in line to meet Carrie Hilson. She was like fourth in line. Andrew just waited as he saw Julissa go to meet her. About 10 minutes later, she comes out with the biggest grin on her face. And her autographed picture. She started talking about how cool she was, and just kept talking. Shows him her pictures with her on her phone.

They both went to the ballet to get his car. The Valley attendant took their ticket, and gave it to another attendant that said, "Okay, so, I am on the way to get your car."

"Okay. Thank you." says Andrew.

All of a sudden. The car drives up and the attendant lady gets out and they get in. Andrew drives her on to her hotel room. He says it was nice to meet her, and have a safe trip home tomorrow.

She says, "Thank you. And be safe going home."

"I will." he says as he drives off.

Julissa then goes downstairs and to her hotel room. She jumps in the shower and finishes packing for her trip home. It is now 12:15 A.M. and she finally climbs into bed and goes on to sleep.

Chapter 8

Home sweet home

The next morning, Julissa gets up a little bit early because she was leaving to go home. It was 8:00 A.M. Her flight was at 1:00 P.M., but she wanted to have some breakfast and do a little more shopping before she had to leave. She gets on up andgets in the shower. Playing some slow jams, and getting all fresh. She was in the shower for quite a while mainly daydreaming. Ready to see Tim. Finally she finishes and gets out and sits on the bed for a few minutes and calls Tim.

The phone just rang and rang and she figured he must be asleep. She then goes back into the bathroom to blow dry, install her hair. She tried to start the blow dryer, but it had a short or something because it wouldn't come on. So listening called downstairs to the concierge to get them to bring her another blow dryer because her hair was still wet, and she did not want to go out looking like that. Waiting on them to bring another blow dryer she gets impatient and decides to go downstairs to see what the holdup was.

She gets downstairs and there are a few police officers at the front desk with some half naked crackhead woman complaining that she was attacked but she couldn't describe the guy because he had on a mask.

The policeman, Mr. Cruz said, "Well, ma'am, we want to help you, but if you have no description we can't really help you."

"He had on a white T-shirt." She says quickly.

And the other police officer Miss Perez quickly says to her, "Ma'am, if we go out there chasing all the men in whiteT-shirts that will be a lot of extra time energy us. And we still might not have the right person."

"Well, y'all need to do something!" Shesays.

"Well, we can file a report, and send you to the clinic to be checked out but then youhave to leave this alone!" Says Mr. Cruz.

"Okay, well I guess" she says.

As all of that died down Julissa goes up to the front desk, and says, "Now, I see whattook so long. Can someone please give me another blow dryer? Please and thank you."

With her hands held out. A few seconds later someone from behind the counter handed her a blow dryer, and said, "Sorry for the inconvenience. If you need anything else please do not hesitate to call back." And as Julissa was walking away Mr.Cruz, one of the officers went at her, with a smile and told her to have a great day! A littleshocked she smiled back and said thank you, you too and went back upstairs.

She goes into her room. Tim calls finally and says he's sorry he missed her call buthe was in the shower, and his phone was on the charger. "Oh, babe, I thought you were probably still asleep."

She says, "Nope, I was in the shower. As I just said, but I did hear the phone."

"Oh, well, I was coming home today Just letting you know, because I thought maybe we would

Netflix and chill tonight ifyou are not too busy or already have plans." Says Julissa

"Yes, of course, I would love that. I just have to do some things today but tonight Iwill definitely love to spend some quality time with you. I've been missing you."

"They took you away for too long." He says.

"Well, I'm sorry but this new position comes with a lot of traveling. We have to make sure I know the ins and outs of my new job. Actually, I will be going back again pretty soon. I have to talk to the boards of all of the states we work with. Financial stuff and making sure everythingis running smoothly with the management teams."

"Damn, again?" Ask Tim.

"Yes, again." Julissa says.

"Well it is your job, so I understand why you have to do it, but this time I will make sure we get to spend more time together before you leave.Or maybe I can go with you or meet you out there. One of the days you're gone? Just a suggestion though. That's if you want me to." Hesays.

"Oh, well, I will keep that in mind. By the way, how is your mom doing?" She askedto change the subject.

"Oh, she is doing well. I talked to her yesterday." He says.

"I'm having lunch with minetomorrow." She says. "Yes, she insisted we have lunch right before I had to go away forthe work days. So that is one thing I have to do tomorrow."

"Mama Lucky must have something really important to talk about." He says.

"Really? Doyou think so?" Asks Julissa.

"Well, yes. You know Mama Lucky. You should know herbetter than me. It's gotta be important, she trying to go and eat and shit." Says Tim.

"I guess I will see you tomorrow. All right then, babe, let me get off this phone, andgo get me some breakfast, and do a little more shopping before I have to go to the airport. You're going to be able to pick me up today right?" She asked.

"Yes, that will be no problem," He says.

"Okay, baby. I will talk to you a little later. Have fun shopping!" Says Tim.

"Okay, I will try to enjoy my few hours left out here." She says and then grabs an outfit out of her suitcase. She picks a cute pair of blue jeans and a T-shirt that she bought last night at the Carrie Hilson concert. It was a white one with her picture, and the words "Pretty Girl Rock" in purple. It was really cute. Mainly because it was her! She got dressed, and then finally was able to do her hair. She straightened it, and then bumped the ends a bit for a fuller body. Grab some gold hoop earrings, and her watch and put them on. She grabbed a black belt, and some Air Force Onesto match her T-shirt. She ended up eating breakfast at Pocahontas Pancake House. She decided on a lobster omelet, and avocado toast. She has seen the reviews and thought that would be the perfect dish. It was a little pricing, but she was falling now so she could enjoy herself on the company's dime, she thought

It wasn't too long that the waitress came to her table with her order. The lobster omelet looks so delicious. The avocado toast was so fresh, and tasted so good. Justlike they had literally taken a spoon, and took all the avocado out and put it on the hot piece of toast. She ate very well, and finished it off with a hot tea.

After eating she took a quick stop at the restroom and went inside to use it. There was a line. She had to go pretty bad so she asked if she could go ahead of them, and they all say there's only one, maybe two stalls. They've been waiting already. They need to go then an older lady suddenly walks out of the stall, and tells everyone she is sorry for taking so long, but she wasn't feeling very good and it just kept coming.

All anyone could do was laugh. The other stall then opens, and another lady comes out. There are two more people in front of Julissa, and soon they are gone. Lily gets to go into a stall, and do her business. As she was sitting her stomach began to hurt, and she then finished up and went to wash her hands, and got out.

It is now 10:00 A.M., and she is not far from the mall, so she decides to take a little walk. She goes to the mall, and goes straight to Victoria's Secret. She saw a bra and panty set she wanted, and then a nighty that she figured she could wear sometime soon. Maybe she would take it with her tonight to go see Tim. It was pretty sexy. She knew he would love it! She looked around a bit more then she walked up to the counter and picked out a new perfume. She also saw a lip gloss that she liked also. The cashier checked her out. Her total came to $103.96.

She handed the lady her American Express. She swipes it and gives it back. The receipt comes out and Julissa grabs it and her bag and leaves the store. She then walks on to the right seeing one of her favorite stores in the distance, beginning to walk in the direction then all of a sudden a guy stops her with a sample of a new perfume, and she says she is not interested, and continues to the store. A few more vendors tried to stop her, but she started getting a little irritated and just picked up her hand letting them know she instantly was not interested, and they left her alone. A little while later she gives it to the store. Looking at her watch. It is now 11:15 A.M. and she needs to find a cute outfit to go and spend a little time with Tim.

She grabs a cute little tank and some tights. Black of course. She hurries to the cashier to check out, but the line is pretty long for a second she was about to go put her things back but she quickly changes her mind, and gets on in line. It is moving pretty fast, so it is not very long before the woman says next and is her turn. She takes her items and lays them on the counter. The lady with the name tag Audrey as if she would like to keep the hangers, And Julissa quickly says "no." Knowing she still needs to pack the things she just bought, she then pays and grabs her bags, and leaves the store.

As she's walking out she looks across and sees a hat that she just has to buy. She goes across and purchases the hat, and looks at her watch and it is now 11:45 am and she knows she needs to get back to her hotel room.

On the way she orders a Lyft ride to pick her up at 12:00 P.M. The airport is only 10 minutes away so she should have plenty of time to get back to the hotel and pack her other items and go. As she gets to her room. She decides to change and put on her new outfit because Time will be picking her up so they might as well just go to his room and chill. She gets back and changes, in packs the rest of her things then goes straight to the front to wait for her ride. As she is waiting she realizes she hasn't checked out of her room, and has a few minutes so she takes her things and goes to do that. When she finishes up she goes back out to wait. Her phone then deans to let her know her ride will be arriving in 3 minutes. As she was waiting, that same crackhead lady walks up, and asked for a few dollars, and Julissais surprised but tells the lady sorry but she doesn't carry cash. The lady made a weird face, and calls her stupid, or something and walks away to a guy close by and ask him the same thing. He says lady go away, and stop bothering people go get a damn job, and stop begging

The crackhead lady said something on her breath and left.

Julissa says, "Oh my, I wish I had something to give her."

He says, "Why? All she isgoing to do is go get high. I see her here all the time, and it's always the samething."

"Ah well, I still just want to help her."

"Lady, you crazy," he says.

"Oh, there is my ride," says Julissa as she grabs her bags and walks toward the black Nissan Maxima. The man gets out and grabs her bags, and puts them into the trunk,and opens the door for her. Then they get in and drive off. He verifies that they are going to the airport, and they head that way. The Lyft ETA says 12:10 and we drive onto the airport. Soon, we make it to the destination and the driver gets out, opens the door, then gets her bags from the back, hands them to her, and thenleaves.

She goes inside and straight to the security line. She handed them her ID, and the ticket was on her phone. They had her go through, and get checked. She grabs her things and goes to her line, and as she is walking to her area she gets a message that the flight is delayed for an hour due to the weather. She gets to a terminal, and sits down. She is sitting a few minutes and then starts to doze off of it. Not wantingto fall asleep she gets up and walks or toward the desk to ask how much longer would the wait be. The stewardess says, "The weather has died down so it will be soon," says the woman.

"Okay, thanks," Julissa says.

About 20 minutes more go by and the person over the speaker is beginning to board the Julissa section. Everyone including Julissa gets up and walks to the line to get boarded. They start to board. Julissa gets up to the front of the line, and poolsher ticket on her phone to get through the line, and it verifies her ticket and sends you through the checkpoint. She then follows the line and gets on the plane.

Waiting for the others to board she calls her mom. Mom answers quickly and says, "Hey, boo bear, Mama going to have to call you back," with the giggle and her voice. Julissa quickly says, "Oh, I was just confirming for tomorrow's lunch."

Mom says, "Of course. Just pick me up at the time we talked about. All right, boo bear. Love you, bye."

Julissa was wondering why her mom sounded like she does when she is busy and trying to get off the phone. Then she really started to wonderwhat tomorrow's lunch was about after thinking about what Tim had said earlier.

Anyways everyone was now boarded, and they started to prepare for take-off. She puts in her earphones and begins to clear her mind. She hated flying but sometimes she would have to for work, so she just closed your eyes and startedlistening to her music.

She zoned out so much that by the time she woke up everyone was preparing to getoff the plane. They had landed, and she had slept through the entire flight. She missed refreshments, and everything. Anyways she grabs her suitcase and gets off too. She goes straight to the pickup area, and Tim was already there waiting for her. He drives up closer, and gets out, and holds the door open for her to get in.

Grabs her suitcase, and puts them into the trunk. They drive off to the hotel andthey get her bag out of the trunk, and go inside.

"I'll take my things to my suite, and then I'll meet you in yours in a little bit." Shesays.

"Okay, sounds great. I need to straighten up a bit anyway." Says Tim.

"Good to go then. Let's meet at your suite in about 30." Says Julissa.

"Okay, no problem." Says Tim as he walks away and goes to his suite.

Julissa goes inside and grabs a drink and goes to her bedroom. While in her room she changes into a comfortable two piece pink short set. Then slipped on her comfy house shoes, and grabbed a robe on the way out of her closet. As she is walking to the living room, she hears the front door, and wondering who has a keyto her apartment, stood in front with a knife.

All of a sudden, she sees Destiny, and says, "Girl, I almost used this knife. Girl, I forgot you were here. I am so sorry." Julissasays looking oh so sorry.

"Oh, yeah, after you said I could stay here till you got back?"

"You just forgot all about little old me," says Destiny with the frown.

"My bad, but in my defense, I was very busy. Flight after flight and meeting after meeting. Busy, busy, busy, my friend. Again I am so sorry but Tim invited me over. It's right down thehall. Can't stay here much longer. I need to go meet with him. It's great to see you."As she gives her a very big hug.

"Oh, well that's okay, because I met someone when I went out one night. Anyway Ihave a date tonight. His name is Julio. He lives about 20 minutes away. So I guess I'll see youtomorrow" said Destiny.

"All right, but I might see you later tonight depending on how the night goes." Julissa says.

"Well, I'm pretty sure I'll be out all night. We have been on a few dates already, andhave been having a great time and a lot of fun since we met, but enough small talk.I need to go. We have a reservation at "Local Motives at 8:00 P.M. Love you, girl.

I'll see you tomorrow." Says Destiny.

"Love you. Have fun! Call if you need me." Says Julissa.

Destiny then goes and showers and gets dressed, and leaves for her date. Julissahad already left and went to Tim's suite.

Julissa knocks, and grabs the door handle, and the door is open. She walks on inside, and Tim says "Hey, make yourself comfortable, babe. I will be right out."

A few minutes later he walks out in some gray sweatpants and a white T-shirt.Looking kind of sexy but Julissa tried not to stare. His package was almost standing at attention. He must have been turned on a bit. She thought.

"Would you like a glass of wine?" Asks Tim.

"Sure, I'll take a glass." Says Julissa. "What movie are we going to watch?"

"I thought we would just pull up Netflix and choose one together. Besides, I have seen a lot of movies. I want to watch something neither of us has watched yet."

"Thatis a great idea."

They start flipping through the movies, and a few flips later they find a good movie. At least its synopsis sounded pretty good. So they decided on it. Tim had already ordered a meat lover's pizza to eat, and just as they start the movie, there is a knock and it is the pizza girl.

Tim opens the door, and she's like, "Damn can I join you?"

Tim says "No! You damn thought. That is so unprofessional," he grabs the pizza and closes the door.

"Ole' girl wanted her some Tim." Says Julissa.

"I didn't want that girl." Says Tim "She was talking all crazy like that was going tohappen. I am here with you and you know you missed me, as he kisses her on the cheek and then sits back down, and presses play.

Julissa is looking like she is a little cool so Tim gets up and goes to the closest to grab a blanket. He lays it over her, and sits back down on the couch next to her. She mentions that he could come closer, and share if he wanted to. He then quicklymoves closer, and slides under the blanket with her.

"Oh my gosh," she says, "your hands are so cold."

"Can you help me warm them?"

"Yes. Depends on how you try to warm them." She says.

"Oh, never mind." He says, "let's justwatch the movie."

They start to watch the movie and after about 20 minutes of watching the first start Julissa starts to fall asleep. Tim not just her to wake her. Shewakes up and starts watching again. They start watching and for about 10 minutes they are both awake then Julissa starts to fall on Tim's shoulders, and falls asleep once more. Again he nudges her and realizes she must be tired, and just lets her laythere. Tim continues to watch the movie and he soon also falls asleep. It is around 12:30 and Julissa's phone rings. She answers and it is the wrong number. Looking at the time. She sees it is getting late.

Tim quickly says, "Don't go. Let's watch a little more of the movie. It's been pretty good. Even though you haven't watched much ofit."

"Okay, that is fine with me." Julissa says and they begin to watch the movie again and aftera couple more minutes both of them fall fast asleep.

Chapter 9

Lunch w/ mom

Julissa woke up the next morning with a headache feeling a little dizzy like she haddrank too much the night before. Why am I not in my bed? She thought.

Tim was in the kitchen making some breakfast. It smelled good. That is what wokeher up in the first place.

"You want some breakfast?" Asks Tim.

"Yes, it smells really good. What are you cooking there?" She asks.

"Bacon, eggs, grits with croissants." Says Tim.

"Yum," says Julissa.

They sit at the table, and eat.

After the meal, Julissa says, "Thank you for the invite, and breakfast.We should do this again soon."

Tim can see his phone on the coffee table ringing. He immediately goes to check it,and the number is unavailable. He just puts it back down and walks away.

It rings again. This time it is Gerald.

He motions to Julissa he needed to take it real quick.

Julissa then goes to the restroom. She really needed to go pee.He answers the phone.

"Hey, bro. How did it go the other night with Aniya? He asks

"Can't talk now bro. Says Tim "I will call you back a little later once Julissaleaves."

"Oh, my gosh. Julissa too. Damn, bro you getting them all. I definitely have to hearabout you and Aniya though" Says Gerald.

"I will call you back." Says Tim.

"Who was that on the phone, babe? It seemed pretty important." Asked Julissa. "Oh, yeah, a little business, babe. We got it right now." He says fumbling all around.

"You ok? You seem nervous." She says.

"Yes, I'm fine." He says.

Looking at the wall seeing it's almost 8:00 A.M. "I have to go get ready to takeMom to lunch."

"And I have to go to a meeting with a potential client of mine with this new ventureI'm working on." Says Tim.

"Meeting with whom, may I ask?"

"Can't tell you right now. I don't want to jinx it, babe. I will give you a little moreinformation once I speak with her."

"Her?" She asked.

"Yes, her! I will get with you a little later after your lunch with your mom." "Well, you didn't have to be so stern with me. I just asked. Okay, well good luckwith your meeting." She says.

"Thanks." He says "I will talk to you later."

"As you mentioned earlier. We need to do this again soon." She says "I would lovethat, but right now I need to go back to my suite. I have been gone for quite a while,and there is no telling what Destiny has been doing! Plus, she should be back by now. She had a date last night." She says as she leaves and goes back to her suite.

Once in her suite, she goes in and gets into bed and rolls over and goes back on to sleep. She didn't have to meet her mom until 11:00-11:30. It is only 6:30 A.M. Shethought. She then goes on back to sleep and wakes up around 8:00 A.M. She is nowa little more refreshed, so she jumps out of bed. She quickly gets up and goes straight to the kitchen and turns on her coffee pot.

Next, she goes and turns on the shower and looks through her closets to find an outfit that she can wear to lunch with Mom. She decides on a cute little pink sundress, and her gold sandals. She figured she would add some gold accessories to Ax in her outfit later. Anyways, she goes back and gets into the shower. She takes about a 30 minute shower. She gets on out, dries offher dripping wet body, and goes to sit down on her bed.

Looking at her cell she sees time is moving quickly, and she needs to call Mom soon. She goes into the family room and sits down on the couch for a bit and shegets a call. Couldn't believe it, Dennis was calling her.

She gives it a few rings then she answers with, "Hey, Dennis, what do you want?"

He quickly says, "I miss you. What did you do to me last night? I waited for youuntil I fell asleep," he says.

She quickly comes back and says, "What do you really miss?"

"Well," She had things to do. Which prevented her from coming over.

He says, "Your smile, your walk, your body. Damn that body! Can I come over andgive you a reminder of how much I miss you?"

"I woke up this morning very excited to touch your pretty face, and it wasn't there," he says.

"Are you drunk, Dennis?" She asked. "'Cuz you certainly sound that way. No, go findyour little yellow sister. I am sure she can make you feel better, or better yet go take a cold shower!" And she hung up

He calls right back and says, "I was not finished. How rude!" And she hung up again.

She quickly gets another call, and she answers and screams. "Will you just give up!" into the phone. Only thing is the person on the other line happens to be Tim.

He says, "Oh, my bad. Give up what?"

She quickly changed her tone and said, "Oh, hey,Tim. What's up?"

"Oh, nothing, just those damn telemarketers calling at the crack of dawn."

"Oh, okay."

Tim says, "I was just checking on you."

"Haven't had the meeting yet, but you were on my mind and I just felt I needed to talk to you."

"Oh, no I am fine." She says. "A little wonder as to what it is, but whatever itis I would just have to understand. That is my mama, and if it is something that willmake her happy I will be happy, too. Well, thanks for checking on me. I need to go and get into the shower, and get a few things done, before I have to go and pick up my mom at 11:30."

"Okay, sweetie, I will be waiting for your call later on, preferably after my meeting. I hope everything goes well and there's no problem." he says.

"Oh, so she's running late?" She asks.

"Why do you say it like that?" He asked quickly.

"Like what?" She asked.

"Like you are jealous, or you are thinking something else." he says.

"No. You're a grown man. You do you," she says, "well it's almost 10:00. I have a little over an hourbefore I need to pick Mom up. I will talk to you later," and she hangs up.

She quickly calls her mom, and makes sure she is up.

She answers on the first ring. "Hey, boo bear. I am up watching my reruns as usual."

"Okay, Mom, I'll see you in about an hour or so." She tells her.

"All right, love. I will see you soon." She says, they hang up and she goes and throwsher clothes on, and goes to do a little light makeup. Nothing too special. It's just mama. Maybe later, I will get a little more jazzed up for dinner with Tom, she thought.

She walks on by the mirror and checks herself out. Damn, I'm sexy, she thought. But she still ended up changing her mind and changed into a blue jean skirt, it was fitting her just right, with pink off the shoulder top. The skirt was a long split up the middle and she was also wearing some pink sandals.

She grabs her keys, and her bag and heads on outside to her car. As she is walking out, she sees Sharon and she is with this fine ass dude that is not Dennis. She givesher a look like, damn, he is fine, isn't he? She smirks 'cuz damn, she doesn't like her. Bitch, please, if I wanted him, I'm sure I could get him. She thought.

She gets into her car and drives off. As she turns out Dennis was coming in with big Joe. He quickly got out of the vehicle, and started yelling at Sharon and grabbed her mother's arm very hard. She quickly stops her car and rolls down her window. Her nosy ass was not going to miss this. She kept hearing Sharon say, "We are not together anymore, Dennis," and trying to get out of his forceful grasp. "I can bewith whoever I want to."

"But not here!" Dennis says.

The guidance says, "Hold up, playboy. The lady says to leave her alone, so I wouldappreciate you letting her go!"

"Or what? What are you going to do?" Dennis asked.

"I'm going to make you!" He commented back.

"Make me, how?" Dennis questioned. And just as he replied, a fist came and hit him inthe lower left jaw.

That guy was not going to let Dennis disrespect his girl. Sharon then says, "Yes,baby. Don't you let him disrespect me like that!"

Dennis comes back at him with a swing, but he misses and the guy grabbed hisarm and pulled him back in a headlock, and tell him to never come near themagain!

Dennis says, "Man, fuck her! Let me go! I am not even trying to fight you, nigga."

He then lets him go and he walks back to his truck and gets in.

"Man, why didn't you help me, Joe?" Dennis says.

"Man, you started that. You disrespected a woman and that is wrong, so I figured you could handle it." Joe says.

"You are my bodyguard. You're supposed to protect me." He explained.

"Yeah, but I also have a daughter, and if you ever disrespected her the way youdid Sharon, I would have punched your ass too."

She looks at the time and it is now 11:20. She quickly puts her car in drive anddrives off to her mom's.

She got there about 15 minutes late, and she was sitting on the porch with a crazylook on her face. She quickly says, "Sorry, I'm late. I was watching a little situationwith my ex-boyfriend, and his old girlfriend, and her new boyfriend. It was so entertaining. My ex got hit in the face!"

"Girl, shut up! I don't want to hear that." She says as she gets in the passenger sideseat, and gives her a hug, and kisses her on the cheek.

"Mom, it was so funny. My ex actually got hit in the face!"

"So, girl. That has nothing to do with me. You just keep dealing with these crazyfolks. Always with some drama."

"Well, Mom I can't help the way others are." She says.

"I know that, baby. I know, but you should do way more research before you make acommitment and you wouldn't be so confused when it all goes wrong." She explains.

"Mom, let's just not talk about it anymore. I knew what I was doing." She tells her.

"Sure, you did, baby." With the sneaky smirk on her face.

The whole time she is driving, Mama Lucky kept texting someone back and forth. She kept grinning from ear to ear,so somebody was making her smile.

She drives on to the restaurant, and they park and go inside. The lady at the frontgreets them with a most beautiful smile, and asks them will it just be the two of them?

She says yes to just the two of us, but then Mom jumps in and says no there willactually be a third meal today. She quickly looks at Mom and says, "Who is thethird?"

"Well, baby, that is the reason that I asked you to come to lunch. His name is LesterRoberts and he is from the south side of Atlanta. We were old friends back in the day, and just recently were able to get back in contact and have been seeing each other for a while now. He is a friend I want to go to college with."

"Okay, I understand how you know him but how long has this been going on? My daddy hasn't been in the gray very long, and you are still here stepping out or waitwas this going on before my daddy died?" She asked.

"Boo bear, there is no way I would have ever cheated on your dad. I love him, withall my heart. We just ran into each other a few weeks after the funeral, and one thing led to another and we decided to start seeing each other." She says.

"Oh, tell me something, I thought I was going to have to go ham over here in thisplace." She says.

"I just wanted to get your blessing first, before we make it official and say we are acouple." She says.

"I'm okay with it, but Alex, I am not so sure. We are going to have to sit him down together. He might understand. Who knows, he might be okay with it? Not! I knowmy brother. At first, he is going to laugh, and say, 'Mom, you're funny! Am I being punked or something?' Then, when he sees you are not kidding. He's going to say, 'Oh, hell no! Ma, what about Dad?'"

"How about we meet at your house tonight?" She says.

"Oh, no. We can't. I kind of have a date with him Tim tonight." She says.

"Well, that is great. Maybe things will work out with you too. Forget that Dennis!" She says.

"Well, how about we sit the meet up for tomorrow at 6:00 P.M." She says.

"Girl, it will not be that bad. Alex can be very reasonable." She says. The waitress came back and asked if we were ready to order our food. They both say yes. She orders her some grilled tilapia with two sides and Mom's orders a shrimpwith salad with ranch dressing. Also ordered another Cosmopolitan.

After the waitress leaves the table, Mom's phone rings and Julissa guesses it's her man, because she answers with, "Hey, baby, what's up? No we changed our minds on the other spot," and told him where they were. "That's great, I will see you in a few minutes."

She looked at her and said, "Wow, was that your plan all along?" She says.

"Yeah, prettymuch. I told you that when we ran into you. He was in the area and said since he isso close, he wants to meet you."

"Huh, sure, Mom. You know He just wants to see you?" She says.

She smiles a big, huge smile and says, "Whatever, boo bear." The waitress comes backwith their food. They hold hands and pray. Once they are done, guess who is standing behind her mother. It's Mr. Wonderful. What a surprise. She thought.

He puts his hands on her shoulders and kisses her on the cheek and says, "Hi, Julissa,is it?"

She says, "Yes, boo bear, is what she calls me."

"Yes, I have heard a lot but she let meknow your real name also," he says.

"Well, hopefully, you got the good version of me, and not the other one." She says.

"Oh,no. She has told me you are a graphic designer for a magazine." He explains.

"Actually, I am the VP right now. I was just promoted a few weeks ago."

"Well I guesscongratulations is an order? So, congratulations!!" He says.

"Thank you." She says.

"Your mom said you were beautiful but didn't say it was a natural beauty. No offense, honey, but your daughter is quite gorgeous." He says.

"None taken." She says, "infact, thank you. She gets it from her mama."

"She sure does, if I may add?" He asked.

"Anyways, enough of the small talk. What are your intentions with my mom? Youbetter not break her heart? She has had enough heartache, and in a very short period of time." She tells him.

"No,sweetie. Definitely not my intention. I want to make her smile and laugh. I want toenjoy her company and vice versa. Take her to places we can see together and oneday if it is possible, marry her." he says.

"You are getting a little ahead of yourself, aren't you? Marriage? Too soon. Too soon!" She says.

"Oh, you know what I mean." He says. "After a little while of dating and things. I am not sure if you understand this, little lady, but neither of us are getting any younger." As he smiles, grabs her hand and kisses it.

"Well, ladies I hate to just pop in and pop out but I have a meeting at 2:00. It was very common. Nice to meet you Julissa but I really must go. You two enjoy the restof your lunch. I hope I didn't rattle any feathers. I will call you later, beautiful." He says.

"Okay," says Mom, then he walks off.

Once he left, Mom started getting all these messages. Julissa asked her who was texting her, and she said, "Oh, it's Les. He sent me asweet text and told me that it was very nice meeting you."

"Les?" She asked. "Tell him, likewise."

"You really mean that, boo bear?" She asked.

"Yes, Mom. He seems like a good fit foryou. And he's a little handsome too. Not a handsome like dad though. He is so polite, and sweet. This may be a good guy. Well, Mom it's almost 2:00. We have been here for a while. Are you ready to go?"She asked.

"Yes, boo bear, we have. And, sure. I have some things to do at the house. Just straighten up a bit. Nothing major but it needs to be done. A little clutter here and there." She says.

"Mom, reallyyou, clutter? That doesn't sound right. I have never seen you leave a cup in the sink, much less dust on the coffee table. He must be taking up all your time." She says.

"Not all." She says with the big smile on her face, "just enough to keep me smiling."

"Smiling? Why are you smiling so hard? You best be on your best behavior mom!I am glad that you are happy again though. Now, it's my turn." She says.

"What about Tim?" She said, "Isn't he making you happy?"

We asked a waitress for thecheck. A few minutes later, she brings it to the table.

I look at the check and quickly take out my American Express and give it to the waitress. She comes back once she puts the card in and brings back the card. She leaves her a nice tip, because she was a great waitress. They get up and go outside tothe car. Get in and continue the conversation.

"Yes, he is Mom. He is a really great guy but something is missing. I'm just not surewhat it is yet."

"Like what boo bear? I hope you are still not thinking about that Dennis boy! He isnot right for you. Listen when I tell you. That boy is hiding something!" She explained.

"Well, he is no longer mine. I don't even care anyway." She tells her.

"Boo bear, I'm mama. I know you, and you can't just let go of your feelings thateasily. I know you still have feelings for that boy! You need closure which younever got!"

"Yeah, yeah, Mom. I am fine! Dennis is old news. I want to work on things with Tim. He is a great guy. We had something great before he left, and maybe he cameback for a real reason this time. We had a nice time last night, and we have a date tonight, so we will see how that all goes."

They get to Mama Lucky's house and she gives her a tight hug, and the sweet kiss on the cheek and says, "Goodbye and I loveyou. Thank you for the advice, but I am okay, Mom."

She then drives off and goes back to her place. On the way she calls Tim. Hope he is finished with his meeting, and he doesn't answer. She gets to the hotel, and Tim's car in the parking lot, but she doesn't see him. She goes on inside and upstairs.First she goes into his sweet spot, and sees if he is there. He is not answering. She calls him again, and he still doesn't answer. At this point, she is really wondering where he is because it is not like him to not answer his phone. She walks onto her suite, and the door is cracked. Nervous about this, she slowly opens her door, and as she does there are rose petals on the floor leading to the bedroom, but there is a note on her couch.

She grabs a note and she reads it and it says look to your right. Well, first close the door, and put what is in the box on. She looks around the corner, and there is a five course meal on the table. State potatoes, mixed vegetables, a roll, and dessert because she can smell a fresh apple pie. Anyways, shegoes ahead and puts on the Versace dress, and heels. It is red lace and all the way see-through. It is beautiful she thinks.

She has on clothes. Suddenly, she hears music playing in the bedroom. She hearsTim say just give me a minute.

He walks in the living room a few seconds after in a three-piece suit with a bow tie.He grabs her by the hand and they walk into the kitchen and he pulls out her chair so she can sit down at the table. He also sits down and says let's eat. He grabs her hand and they pray.

When done, they begin to eat. He grabs a knife in a fork and cuts her steak for her. Then he feeds her a few pieces. There was steak sauce dripping down her chin, andhe quickly jumps up and comes to her face and wipes it off.

"Can't have you messing up that dress can we?"

She smiles and says, "Well, thank you."

He says, "It's my pleasure."

After a little while they finished their dinner. Having one of their best conversations in a long time. He tells her to get ready for dessert. He opens theoven and takes out the apple pie and goes into the freezer for some ice cream.

"Wait here, I need a few more minutes." He says.

"Okay. Just hurry up." She says.

He agrees and walks to the bedroom with his hands behind his back. It is dark toward that direction so she can't see anything from where she is. She looks around the corner, and finally he is coming back. He has a blindfold and he pulls it over hereyes. He then grabs her by the waist and steers her in the direction he wants her to go. I am not sure how far we have walked but I think we are in the bedroom. There is a sexy aroma, and it feels good in here.

He takes the blindfold off of her face and all she can see is candles. He has set up in a beautiful arrangement, and he walks behind her and slowly unzips her dress. He kisses her back and down her spine. She feels something cold run down her back. She shivers but he loves it. He puts ice cream on her back. He quickly licks up the ice cream and pulls down her dress a little more and drops it to the floor. Turns her around and leans her back onto the bed.

He kisses her ever so gently and it made her body week. He goes down to her neck and sucks in all the right places and continues down to her shoulders. He kisses each shoulder and licksdown to her breasts. He sucks her left nipple and then onto the right. He grabs both and pushes them together, and nibbles on them at the same time. This makes her body so hot. She starts getting warm in her vagina area. He must sense this becausehe then slowly puts his finger in her vagina and starts to play with it. Seeing how her body reacts, he follows with another and pushes them both deep inside right, onher clit.

She moans in the deepest pleasure, and soon he puts his tongue on her belly button and licks a little and moves right where she wants him to go. He has his tongue begin to outside and make her squirt everywhere. He grabs a spoon of ice cream and puts it on her vagina. She quickly jumps. It is freezing cold. Her vagina is so cold but then his tongue follows the ice cream, and her body warms upreal quick. He holds her down while he's licking off the ice cream and she is almost screaming.

He's eating her like he was hungry, and she was his plate. He put the tongue up inside all his mouth. Then goes in again. Her body feels so good. She can't even be still. She starts to pull away, and he grabbed him pulls her back toward the bottom of the bed. She moans in pleasure and he just keeps on licking.She is truly trying to get away from him at this point. Her body is so extra sensitive, and finally he lets go. This man got her over here crying. He now flips her over and puts his feet inside of her and just pushes all the way, but at first it is slow.

He starts to go faster, and she feels like she's about to literally come right this moment. She grabbed the shoulders and pushed back. It feels like she's about to explode. She is not ready to come yet but oh gosh. It is coming whether she wants it to or not. She now holds on tight to his shoulders, andlets it go. She screams I am coming, as it begins to slowly lose out. It feels so damn good and she can't control herself. Her body tenses all up on him and he looks into her eyes as he also tenses up himself. His eyes wrote back in his head, literally and he kisses her on her lips and tries to excite her body some more.

He's now has her wanting more, but he looks tired. He looks over to the table and grabs the apple pie and begins to eat it. The ice cream he had was melted, and the apple looks so good. He gets a spoonful and feeds it to her. It is still hot, and almost burns her mouth. But it tastes so good though. Maybe, he will be a keeper after all.

She thinks to herself. He knows all the things I like. I'm sure he remembered a fewthings from the past but as long as he made my body feel this way every time, thenwe would be good she thought. He finished up his piece of apple pie and ice creamand took the dishes to the kitchen. When he gets back to the bedroom, she is laid across the bed. Her body was so exhausted she tried to keep her eyes open, but it was so hard. "Are you going to your room tonight or are you staying here?" She asked.

"I'm staying here, babe." He smiles and says.

"Good. That makes me happy!" She says, "Oh yeah, how did your meeting go? Or do you not want to talk about it now?"

"Oh, we went pretty well, 'she' actually ended up being a guy, instead. She called the head and said she wassending him to her place."

"Oh, so, she didn't show up?" She asked.

"No, the meeting went pretty well."

He then grabs her and hugs her and they cuddle until they fall asleep.

Chapter 10

My Sunday

It is like 3:00 A.M. now. Julissa wake up. It's been about an hour. She was up and horny again trying to figure out how she could wake him. Should she wake him up, or shouldshe pretend she is asleep and have him wake her? She really didn't know how he would prefer it to go down, so she just kissed him on his lips, and he tasted hers. It woke him up.

She kissed him all the way down to his chest and his stomach. She proceeded to move further down now that she did, he grabs my head on both sides and guides me to his liking. Julissa slowly stroke his manhood and get him excited, and she put it in her mouth. He moans and smiles as he watches her go down on him. Every stroke he clenches up his whole body and she can feel it with her mouth goes back down. She use her hand for a little while because her mouth gets tired, and he quickly asked for the mouth again. This time he stays really tense for quite a bit, and as she have her mouth on the two, he grabs her hand and wants her to stroke as she sucks and after a few seconds he ejaculates all in her mouth.

They had never done that before. Usually, she moves out of the way, but he was holding her head so tight that she couldn't help but swallow. It was so nasty! All salty, and she almost threw it back up, but she held it in. Hethen just lays there enjoying that feeling. She quickly tells him, "Don't do that again!"

He says, "Why not?"

"Because it's nasty and I don't like feeling like I'm about to throw up." She says.

"Oh, you are fine." He says.

"Actually I'm not, but let's just not do that again." She explains.

"Oh, okay, whatever you say, babe. I will not hold your head. I'll just let you please your man. You knowthat is what I like though, baby. Can't you just let a brother enjoy it once in a while?" He asked

"It depends on you, love." She says.

They lay down to get more comfortable, and not long after they are both asleep again. About 5:00 in the morning. She jumps up and gets into the shower feeling soicky, but in a good way? Last night was amazing. She thought, he still knew how tosatisfy her every need.

It was a quick shower, and she jumped on out. He is sound asleep still. She thought,guess I can say I did that! She thought with a huge smile. Oh well, I am hoping for a nice time with him, but who knows what God has instore for us. She also thought.

She had to go to work in a few hours, so she just put on a pot of coffee to wake herup. As it was brewing, it smelled so good she easily started to wake up. Asthe coffee was brewing on the stove she turned on the television. She sat there for a little bit, watching, and then could feel hands on her shoulders and a voice saying, "Good morning, baby. Howdid you sleep?"

She tells him, "I slept good."

He says, "Baby, if you don't mind I'm going to take a shower before I leave."

The coffee pot finishes, and she jump up quickly to go and grab a cup. She adds some cream and sugar. That is how she likes her coffee. She asked Tim would he likea cup, and he passed. Saying I will get one, once I get out of the shower, as he walks to the bedroom.

She sat back down on the couch and enjoyed hers. She turned the channels until she got to the news. She sits there watching for a bit then she realizes she's still in her towel, and she needs to get dressed for work. She had only had this position fora few weeks but it certainly would not be good to be late. She thought.

She finishes up for coffee and she has to go to the bedroom. She looks in her closet, and grabs a pair of khaki pants, and a white top. She didn't want to dress up today. She just wanted to go to work and try to keep Mr. Michael out of her mind. Hopefully, today she doesn't really have to deal with him. He really was mad at her,but honestly Mr. Prince put her in a very bad situation, she thought.

Shake it off, Julissa! Get him out of your mind. He is not important right now. You just need to focus on doing your job and taking care of all of your other clients. Shethought to herself.

She grabs her clothes and lays them out on the bed.

Tim is still in the shower, so she goes and grabs another cup of coffee. These thoughts of Dennis keep going through her head. She just needs to go and find some way to distract her mind from these thoughts. She hears the water in the shower, and she decides to go and join Tim. The water is steaming up the bathroom.

He then looks over the top of the steam and says, "babe, sorry, I know you need totake one too, but it just feels so good that I didn't want to get out, but you are welcome to join me." He says.

"No, I'll pass. I have already taken mine. Don't you see me in this towel."

"Oh, I just thought you were about to take a shower." He says. "Well, plus, that barter looks kind of hot."

She says, "By the way, I thought you liked it hot?"

He says, "Yes. I do, but that seems harder than usual."

"I'm okay." She says.

She walks into the living room and starts watching TV some more. A few minuteslater Tim comes out with nothing but his towel and stands in front of her, manhoodhanging with the big-ass grand on his face!

"Babe. Damn that shower felt good." He says.

She quickly looks up at him, and says, "Damn, babe, what time is it?"

He looks at the clock on the wall and says, "Almost 7:30. Why?"

She screams, "Oh shit!" And quickly jumps up and goes and grabs her clothes and putsthem on.

She doesn't even put on makeup because she has already wasted enough time. Shequickly throws her clothes on and heads downstairs.

And she is walking to the elevator, she sees Dennis, and he is all dressed up, withsome suits in his hand walking toward the elevator.

"Why are you up so early?" She says to him.

He says, "I got a call from Mr. Prince yesterday saying to be in the office thismorning for headshots to be taken."

"Well damn, this is the first I had heard of this information." She thought.

She quickly texts her emails, and there are about three from Mr. Prince. Saying. "There is a new campaign coming out next month and we need Mr. Dennis. Some newheadshots and other pictures taken ASAP! The next one is labeled important!"

She opens it and it says we have a meeting today at 10:00 A.M. with corporate. No explanation just that it is an urgent matter. Dennis is talking but she is completely blocking him out.

"Oh. Miss Lucky?" He says.

"What do you want Dennis?"

"How are things with your new boo?" He adds.

"Huh," I said. "What boo?" Acting all innocent like I had no idea who he was referringto.

"That dude you were with the other day." He asks.

Looking like he's no big deal. She says, "Oh, Tim, but I wouldn't exactly say boo, butwe are okay. It's none of your business anyway, Dennis!"

"Yes, you are right," he says.

"None of my business."

"Well, I guess I will see you around the office, Miss Vice President." He says.

"Yes, I am sure you will." She says she looks up at him. "I am the new VP." Damn thathas an amazing ring to it, she thought.

He didn't say a word. He just gave me the most disgusting look and walked off.

She left too, and then she was on her way out to her car anyways. She gets in and wonderedwhy Mr. Prince didn't inform her of that little photo she would take with Mr. Michaels. She almost pulled out in front of some lady going entirely too fast through theparking lot.

Not sure who she is, she just waves her off and apologizes.

She quickly drives off, not too long after, she gets to the office. As she is goinginside, of course, again, she runs into Dennis.

If I didn't know any better. I would say he was finding me on purpose, but we dolive and work in the same place, so it's possible. She thought.

Oh well, she gets on the other day and as Dennis stopped by our now, new photographer, Angela. She surely would have thought that Mr. Prince would have given that job to Jeremy. He dabbled a little in photography, and plus he is way more dependent. Angela is good at her job, but she is very seldom here because sheis a mom of two boys, and she is always calling off.

Anyways, if she doesn't get it right, I will put in a good word for Jeremy. Maybe Mr. Prince will consider him. She thought.

She gets on the elevator and goes on to her new office next to Mr. Prince. He is inhis office, and currently on a call as she knocks on his door. He motions for her towait a few minutes. She goes on to her office, and turns on her computer and triesto catch up on her emails. Once she is on, she sees an email from Carol.

Carol was one of her friends from college. She is just reaching out and telling her that she will be coming into town in a few days. She looks over at the calendar andsees that this was a few days ago, and she will be flying in from Africa tomorrow, at noon. She quickly emails her back and tells her she can't wait to see her, and she will be there by noon to pick her up.

All of a sudden she popped up on video chat, and looking just like the bad bitch she always was. She says to her, damn where you haven't changed a bit I see you outin Africa killing them.

Anyways to explain her more in detail, she was a journalist for finesse magazine. You both decided to go with the magazine. She was a triple threat. Shehad the beauty, the brains and the personality to match. She was such an amazing friend, she is my ride or die from way back. She was doing a very big story the pastmonth or so, so I tried not to bother her, but I guess she must be done

We spoke for a few minutes. I guess I was a little too loud, and Mr. Prince motionedover for me to now come see him.

I quickly hang up with Carol and rush into his office. He says, "Julissa, I need you to monitor the photo shoot for Mr. Michaels. Angela is good, but, of course, I need youto make sure she is great! After that, I need you to go and fire Dean Brass. He has been in the news since this morning about a rape case. He was out with some girl, and she screamed great, and is all over Atlanta today. He has been a great asset to this magazine, but you know how I feel about that publicity. I cannot have this magazine all over the news in a bad light. As of today, he will no longer be anemployee here."

She looks at him all funny, like really, and he says, "That is all for now. If I need you Iwill call you, or just come find you myself."

She doesn't even argue. She just goes on to the photo shoot and does as she is told.She gets on the elevator and goes to our photography studio upstairs. Once she is there, she goes inside, and tells Angie to pause because she needs to talk to her.

She says, "Dennis Michaels will I speak to Miss Lucky."

He says, "Oh, no problem. I will go on a bathroom break and grab a snack."

"Okay, whatever," she says.

"Well, Angela, I need you to do these particular shots." As Julissa shows her a template ofwhat they need in order to make sure the advertisement looks great.

She says, "Okay, that would not be a problem at all, Miss Lucky."

"Also, I need you to have him change into another outfit for those sets. We are marketing this brand, and he was wearing their clothing. I need you to go and findsomething back there that they have sent us and get him changed and ready in a few minutes. I am not about to have you taking pictures all day! We have many more things to do with him!"

"Yes, ma'am. Right away," she says.

"I will be here to watch, and if you need to change anything, I will be sure to let youknow. Now, get him back in here, so we can relate the information and we can get started."

"I will go now, Miss Lucky." She says.

As Angela is walking out of the room, Dennis is coming in, and she starts talking to him. She shows him his clothes, and he quickly grabs new clothes and hurries to get changed. A few minutes later, he comes out looking sexy in a pair of shorts with the tank top.

She's remembering how this man looks naked and that makes her extra smiley. As Angela started taking the pictures, she started fantasizing. She was thinking about them on a deserted beach somewhere in Florida. She was putting fancy moves all over his body and rubbing it in very well.

As she is running it in, she can hear a woman calling her name and it suddenly became clear that it is Angela.

"Miss Lucky, Miss Lucky, how do you like the shots I've done so far?" She asked.

She just says, "Great, Angela. Just what we wanted. Do me a favor and print a few samples, so I can show them, to Mr. Prince."

"Sure. It will only take me a few minutes." Says Angela.

"Okay." She tells her.

After about 10 minutes, she brings the samples back, and she quickly leaves. She was so ready to get out of there. The heat from her while looking at Dennis was going to get her into trouble.

She begins to think. I know Mr. Prince said to stay and wanted to supervise but with these daydreams I am having about him, I just needed to get out of there. She leaves and goes to the floor, where Dean works.

She passes him and says to him, "What are you about to do?"

He says, "On my way out to lunch with a friend."

I don't tell him what I was told to do, instead, I just say, "Okay," and walk on down the hall. Postponing it for later. I am sure he will thank me later, she thought

She walks on back to Mr. Prince's office, and before she knocks, he says just to come in. She does, and he says, "Well, is it done? Did you fire him yet?"

She tells him, "No, not yet."

She hands him the samples, and he loves them.

He says, "Don't be trying to change the subject! The quicker the better. He knows the rules and regulations of this establishment, so he should already be prepared. He knows I see and hear everything."

"Mr. Prince, I would do it just as soon as he gets from lunch. As I passed through the hall earlier, he was on his way out to lunch with a friend."

"Okay, but if it's not done today, you might just be in another position by morning," he says.

I securely say, "Dang, Mr. Prince. I will do it! Please do not make those kinds of threats. I love my job!"

He says, "Well, if you love it so much, do it, and the best way you know how. Now, I said fire Mr. Sprawls. I need it done ASAP!"

"Yes, Mr. Prince as soon as he gets back. Not a problem."

"Good girl," he says, and motions for me to get out of his office.

She goes back to her office and does a little paperwork that was sitting on herdesk. She looks at the time. It is lunch for her, but she will wait until Dean gets back and do what she needs to do, and then go tolunch. She continues with the paperwork. It was a pretty big stack of papers she had to sign because of her new position, and plus a packet, with the instructions for Mr. Michael's meetings.

Damn, dude was not kidding. I thought. She got a text from Tim asking if she would befree for lunch, and of course, Julissa had to text back telling him no, because she had to wait for this guy to fire him. She didn't tell him but she knew why.

He quickly sends her back a sad emoji, and says, well I guess I will see you later atthe suite tonight.

She texted him back. "Okay, babe."

After another 30 minutes or so, Dean walks back onto the floor.

Julissa called him into her office. He quickly comes to her office and she asks him toshut the door.

Mr. Prince is looking all hard and being very nosy. She explains to Dean how goodhis work has been here, but she says, we have to let you go!

He asked, "Why? What did I do? If I may ask?"

As if he didn't know already. And she says to him, "Mr. Prince does not want to have todeal with bad publicity. The rape charges that you are under investigation for, we want no part of. If you think this is unfair then you are happy to read the information in your application with all our rules and regulations, and bad publicitywill definitely be one of those things we do not tolerate!"

Not that it will change his mind, but just wondering in case we do get a bunch ofquestions anyway.

"I didn't rape that girl! She was mad because I wouldn't give her money for her rentand she hit her leg after we had sex, and it looks like it was forced rape because wehad just had sex and she used it to her advantage. It was consensual. She wanted the sex but when I didn't give her the money, she screamed right and I guess a neighbor called the police. It was a girl I have been sleeping with for a few months."

"So, you didn't do it? That is good to hear. I hope everything works out, andif you get cleared. I will see what Mr. Prince has to say." She tells him.

"I understand the policy butplease, I can't be fired. I have bills to pay." He pleads.

"I'm so sorry, Mr. Sprawls, but please leave. I have a lot of work to do. I wish you luck with your next job, and we will help you in any way we can." She says.

He leaves her office, and she goes over to Mr. Princes' office and he says, "The job is welldone! That's the kind of VP I need!"

"If there is nothing more that you need right now, I'm about to go to lunch." She tellshim.

He says, "How about you take the rest of the day off? You can look over the rest tomorrow. I will text or call you, if anything comes up that we need your help with."

She says. "Thanks so much Mr. Prince." She really needs to go home and get ready for her friend

Kera to come tomorrow. "By the way I will need to either be off tomorrow or be off by 11:00 to go and pick her up from the airport."

"I will do what I can. I will let you know for sure about tomorrow morning beforework." He says.

"Thank you, Mr. Prince. I really appreciate it." She tells him.

"Well, just do your job and there will be plenty more days of appreciation." He says.

"I like the sound of that. Cool, no problem." She says as she walks out the door. She gets to her suite. She opens the door and Tim is sitting on the sofa watchingTV. She quickly tells him about Kera coming to visit tomorrow.

He says, "That is great I know how close you two were back in the day."

She tells him, "Yes, babe. I miss her so much. We haven't really seen each other forabout a month. We have a lot of catching up to do. Maybe you can give us a fewdays. Instead of you staying here you can stay in your sweet home?"

"Oh, yeah. I understand. I can catch up on some things there. And I will see youwhen I see you." He says.

"What do you want for dinner?" She asked.

"I don't know, baby. What do you have in mind?" He asked.

"How about we go out for dinner?" She says.

"Yes, that sounds good. I really didn't feel like cooking tonight," he says.

"How about we go to this place I heard of from a coworker, called Shay Lujan?"

"Okay, that sounds good."

"I guess we can leave in about an hour. Early dinner withthe late night." He says with the big ass grin on his face.

We both get dressed and leave for the restaurant. As we get there, we go in and sit down. This was our first time going to this place. Shay Lujan was beautiful. The decor was exquisite. As you walked in there was purple drapery over the windows.Black walls with yellow lighting. The tables had gold tablecloths with printed centerpieces.

Tim looks at me and says, "This place was a great choice, babe."

We ordered our food and talked a little more. The waitress was so nice, and she suggested we get some shrimp etouffee as an appetizer with some bread. We agreed, and she left the table. Tim and I just said a little longer and waited on ouradvertiser. Soon Julie, our waitress, showed up and said it would be about five more minutes. They wanted it to be hot and fresh.

They both ordered lobster tails, and just said they're talking about this and that andeating their roles on the table those roles were delicious. Tim asks, "Why did you make such a big deal back in the day, when I wanted to go tothe Marines?"

Her face quickly went from a smile to a friend. Not really wanting to talk about this right now, but he deserves to know the truth, so she tells him. Because she knewshe would lose him. She was just being selfish, and she is sorry.

Tim says, "Yes, life has been great since I enlisted. I got my college paid for, and all with the military. They truly took care of me. I have seen the world, and thanks to you been able to experience life with other women, as you started laughing out loud. You had really pissed me off with their selfishness. A lot could have been different in both our lives. Yes I would have still enlisted in the Marine Corps, but we would have built a life together instead of a part. I'm sure we would have been married with kids and living somewhere amazing."

She quickly tells him, "I know, I know, please, just let it go!"

He says, "You would probably own a magazine company rather than be working for one. You have always been the one with the smarts. Straight A's all through school. Just a beautiful, smart and loving person."

"Oh, well, aren't you sweet? Can we just talk about something else?" She tells him.

"Okay, how is your mom?" He says.

"She is doing fine. Not at 100% but she is much better now that how she was at first."

"Yes, when I saw her, she was definitely not herself," he says.

"Well, now she has a new man. His name is Lester. They seem very happy. I'm sure no one is the same. Dad is the one who kept everything together. He was the rock of the family, and I truly miss him." I say, as a teardrop fell from the corner of my right eye. We talked a little more, waiting for the food to arrive. The food arrived not too much later, and we began to eat.

I have never eaten lobster tails before, so I watched him start to eat his first, and kind of followed suit. He started tearing into his like it was the last supper. Oh my gosh, just a mess over there. She shook her head.

He looks at her eating all cute, and he says, "Girl, you better eat or else I will finish it for you. I'm not paying all this money for you to just play over your food." He says.

They finish their food eventually, and clean up their hands and both go to the restroom to clean up a bit better.

She comes out of the restroom first, and then sits patiently waiting as the waitress comes up and takes the plates off the table and asks if we would like any dessert?

She tells her, "No. We are okay."

She continues cleaning the table and walks away.

Tim comes out of the restroom, and says, "Babe, are you ready?"

I say, "Sure. I'm just going to finish up this wine, and I will be walking out." She says.

"I'm going to go up front and pay the check. By the time I am done you should be ready, right?"

"Yeah, okay. I should be. As she smirks up her lip as if he is trying to rush her. "You know what, how about we get some dessert first?" She suggests.

"You sure, babe?" He asked.

She says "Sure, I got a little taste for something sweet. At first I didn't want dessert but now, I do."

He says "There is nothing sweeter than, you, love."

He goes back to the table and orders some cheesecake. A cherry for him and astrawberry for her.

She looks at him all crazy, and he says "What? I'm not supposed to remember yourfavorites? She just says, "Oh my, that is amazing that you still remember after all these years?"

He says with so much swag, "You never forget your first love, Julissa!"

She can feel her body getting so wet, as he smiles and she gets chills all over herbody! Wow! She thinks as she smile back.

They sit in the waitress and bring the cheesecake. They eat their delicious cheesecake, while they offer their confidence to the ship once they are finished.Best cheesecake they had ever tasted! They both said to the waitress.

The whole time she was thinking and wanting this man to just grab her and kiss her,and put his hands all over her body. Hell, she wished she had saves and cheesecake to eat off her body once they got home.

Damn, I was thinking as I looked down and saw I still had a bit of wine in myglass.

She asked him, "Are you ready to go now?"He says yes.

He got up and went to pay the check, and I hurry and drink up my wine, and I amthere right before he is done.

"Perfect timing." He says.

We walked out to the car and got inside. It was so warm there that the restaurantwas kind of chilly.

He asked, "What would you like to do now?"

"I usually would just go back to my room, and watch TV till I fall asleep, buttonight is much different. How about we go see a movie?"

"Okay," Tim says. "What is playing?"

"I'm not sure," she tells him. "Well, let's go and see," he says.

"Sounds good to me." She tells him.

They drive over to the movie theater, and both get out and see what is playing. There are a few good ones, but nothing started for another hour or so. We figuredout the movie that we will watch.

He pays for two tickets, and quickly suggests that we take a walk in the park.Saying it will help us waste time rather than just sitting in the car waiting.

She says, "Okay, sounds like a great idea. It is so pretty outside tonight."

He grabs her hand, and they walk on in the direction of the park. It wasn't very far.Just a block down from the theater. They get to the park, and it is pretty, and very quiet. It's only us, and there is just a little breeze. Just enough to feel a little cool. They walk and talk about things. Things that they had tried to get out of their heads, but still found a way back in. He pulls her clothes, and kisses her and she really likes it.It felt like old times. Oh my, and he was a great kisser then as he is now.

He made her body excited even in the places she had forgotten about.

They continue the kiss for what seems like eternity, and she stops him because it'sgetting her very excited. If we had gone any longer we were going to be in these trees somewhere. She's thinking.

No, not really. I'm not that kind of girl. Shame on you for believing that. She immediately thinks to herself afterwards. Anyways, they walked back to the theater, and they still had a few minutes till the movie started so they grabbed some popcorn, and sodas. Of course, she also had to grab some sugar baby candy. Those are so good, but not good for her. Too much sugar, but every time she comes to the theater, she just has to get a box. Well if you all were wondering we picked a romantic comedy called mysterious by Darlene McCall. She was some not so familiar author and producer.

The movie was good. It was about this woman who was mysteriously planning on taking over the building that she worked in, with her best friend. It was a comedy. We left so hard and couldn't stop the whole movie. We didn't finish the movie, and we went to the nearest ice cream parlor, and got some ice cream cones. We get back in the car and eat our ice cream. We decided to sit and eat it before leaving. Because we knew it would be very messy.

She's just sitting kind of in a daze, and Tim asked, "Baby, what's on your mind? You haven't even eaten hardly any of your ice cream. Something must be bothering you. Tell Timothy what is pondering in that pretty little mind of yours!"

"Nothing," She says. "The ice cream is just so cold. I'm just taking my time."

"Oh, okay," he says. "Well, if you had something to tell me, you would right?"

"Of course, you know I don't bite my tongue."

She then asked him to take her home. "I'm really tired, and just want to go and layin my bed," she says.

He says, "That is fine, and he drives on to the hotel."

He walks her in and up to her suite. Give her a goodbye kiss, and ask, "Can I come in for a minute? Because I need to use the bathroom."

I say, "Okay, that is cool," and he goes to the restroom.

It was extra cold for some odd reason. I guess I had turned off the heat before I left. I quickly turned it back on, grabbed the big blanket I had in the closet, and sat down on my bed. She's just waiting for him to leave so she can take off her clothes and jump in the shower.

Tim comes out of the restroom, and sees me on my bed and comes right on in. He grabs a remote and starts flipping through the channels.

"Sir, what are you doing?" She asked. "Thought I would see what's on," he says.

"Oh no." She tells him, "I need to relax tonight."

"Okay, babe Do you have anything to drink?" He asks.

"Why? Because you were supposed to be leaving?" She asked him.

"A man can't have a drink first?"

"Sure about water. You can go you can take one to go," she tells him.

"That is so rude, Julissa." he says, "what about some crowns?"

"No, I don't think liquor would mix well with the ice cream we just had." He agrees and goes to get a lot of water.

He came out of the kitchen and looked toward my bedroom again. I told him. Ithought you just needed to use the restroom?

"Yes, but I saw you in here looking all sexy inside to come and give you another kissgoodbye." He says.

"Okay, then you will need to go. I am tired. It's been a very long day!" She says. "Okay, okay that is it."

He reaches down and grabs my face and rubs it ever so gently, and kisses me so subtly that everything in me just wakes up.

She grabs him and pulls him in closer as they fall into the bed. His kisses areamazing, and he moves to my neck. He goes to the sensitive part.

He remembers all of the ways to get me completely aroused. She thought

I am just in all as he kisses my neck again, and now moves toward my chest biting my nipples just how I like it. Just hard enough to excite my other parts. He bites each nipple and as he is making me moan, he slides his finger into my vagina. I begin to moan even harder. He keeps pushing them inside and slowly takes them all the way out, watching as my cream drifts between his fingers. He turns me overand continues to push them inside of me, and the more I mowing the faster he moves them. He slowly puts his penis into my vagina. We were now in my favorite position which was doggy-style. He already knows I am highly aroused, so he starts going fast and ramming his big cock inside of me. It feels so good, and all I could do is hold on to my headboard as he moved in and out and in and out makingmy throat, making me throw my ass back into him.

He feels just like always. That man can put it down in the bedroom, she thought I am never unsatisfied when he makes love to me. He starts to moan as I am thinking he is about to ejaculate. He grabs my ass so tight and really begins to give it to me. Stroke after stroke he gets louder, and he ejaculates all inside of me. It just keeps coming and I could tell because he didn't let go of my ass. He lets out one last moan and falls back onto the bed.

I climb on top of him trying to make sure he is good, and he just says stop! He keeps jumping because his manhood is so sensitive. I keep on touching it, and hejust turns his back to me, and just lays there trying to catch his breath. He turns back around, and whispers to me that he missed me and I just made him so happy. She smiles and she agrees that she has missed him too, and they just lay there holding each other as they are still catching their breaths.

After a few more minutes they both close their eyes, and drift off into sleep.

Chapter 11

Kera comes to Atlanta

Julissa wake up kind of early because today her girl, Kera, is coming, and I had a few things to get done before she shows up. She goes and takes a quick shower and throws on a cute little outfit. Goes into the kitchen and puts on her regular daily pot of coffee. Caracalla's and makes sure everything is good and she can pick her up fromthe airport.

Of course, she tells her, "Just make sure you do not miss your flight." She says, "I'll be there early in case you end up making it in earlier than planned."

"I am so excited to see you, and make sure you tell your mom I will notleave without coming to see her."

"I will tell her as soon as I get off with you. I know she will be extra excited to seeyou."

"Awesome, love. I will see you soon. Love you, girl."

"Love you, too, Kiki." I say as Ihang up the phone.

It is about 7:00 A.M. She calls her mom and gives her the great news. She tells herKera is going to be here today around lunch time.

"Oh my, that is great! I cannot wait to see her!" She says.

"Well, Mom, I was just giving you a heads up. Love you and we will see you later once she gets here." She tells her.

"Sounds good, boo bear. I will be looking forward toit. Maybe, she can meet Lester, too. He will be coming by for dinner."

"Oh, yeah, another thing, Mom. Alex has a new boo and he wants us all to meet hervery soon. He asked me to ask you to cook dinner. She has twin girls. He seems really serious!"

"Damn, Alex and a woman with kids? I might just need to cook to get to see this formyself." She says.

"Oh, okay, Mom. Sounds great I will tell him you said you will cook."

"Do you know when will be a good night? I am thinking sometime before Kera leaves because she will not believe it either unless she sees it for herself."

"Yes, I know Kera will be so surprised. Well, I am not really sure how long sheis staying. We never really talked about all that yet. She will be here a little later today." Mom is like.

"Been over a month since I have seen her."

"Yes, boo bear, actually that is the same for us all, but I understand what you're saying." She says.

"Yes, Mom. I can't wait to go out with her, and just enjoy ourselves." She tells her.

"Don't be goin' having too much fun. I know how you two get when you aretogether! You got a man now and you better not go out and mess that up!" Shesays.

"Mom, we don't have titles as of right now. We are still trying to figure thingsout, but you're right, I don't want to mess this up. I know, Mom, and I want that. I really care about him. I honestly think that he is theone that got away, and I cannot wait to see how true my thoughts really are." She says.

After that she quickly wraps up the call and get started. It is almost 7:45 and she just needs to get so much done before Kera shows up. Sheneeds to do a little shopping, straighten up the sweets, and go to the bank.

She quickly gets on up and gets going. She walks out to her car, and of course, she runs into Dennis. He is on his way up to his suite. As she passes by him, he slapson her ass and says, "Damn girl! It is getting bigger? Shit, oh, boy must be hitting that right?"

She turned and said, "Don't you ever hit me like that again. You lost your privileges for this ass when you wanted to act a fool. I am good now. Just know this!" She says.

He then made the most disgusted looking face and walked off mumbling under his breath. She walked on to her car and drove one to the bank. A couple of minutes later she drives up to the bank and gets out and goes inside. She handles her business, and in a hurry gets out of there. For a change it was not even that busy.

Usually she walks in and just wants to walk out. There are so many people there. She drives onto the grocery store and grabs some things that they can make duringthe week while Kera is visiting. She moves through there kind of fast because she knows she has a lot of cleaning to do once she gets back home.

As she is leaving, she runs into Mom's guy friend, and he speaks and goes on. He must have been in a hurry, because he was really rushing. She goes on to the suite and begins pulling off the groceries she just bought. Once that was finished, she remembered she needed to wash some clothes, so then goes and puts a load of jeans in the washing machine. She then pours her a glass of wine and goes into her room and picks up a bit. She knew she had made a mess this morning getting ready, but she did not know if it was this it was as bad. She had clothes all over the bed, and the floor. She finishes in there, and heads to the bathroom. It was not quiteas bad. Just needed to clean the shower, and around the sink.

Quick job then she headed to the kitchen. There were a few dishes, but not much to do in there either. She usually kept her kitchen looking decent. She washes dishes as soon as she's finished cooking. She then walks into the living room and see the remote on the floor, so she pick it up and lay it on the coffee table. Completely confused by how it got there, but oh well now the suite is cleaned up and she still have a few hours before Kera is playing is due to arrive at the airport. She starts to read a story on hertimeline and all of a sudden Dennis pops up on her messenger.

He says, "I saw you online, and I just wanted to apologize for earlier. I did not think I had done anything wrong until I saw your reaction, but you walked off so pissed off I didn't think to say sorry at that very moment."

She replies and says, "I accept your apology.Now, leave me alone!"

"Why are you not at work?" He asked.

She said, "None of your business! You just needto be doing what you are supposed to do. I am sure you do not have time to be here."

"Well, I am not working today either. Mr. Prince gave me the day off. He said I needed a little break. You were not coming in so I might as well just relax today. Idid not argue with the man. I left and came back here to my suite, and now I amjust chilling at Boss's orders." He says.

"Whatever, Dennis. I do not care. I have things todo." She say and get off messenger.

It is now a little bit closer to me having to leave, so she go and grab another glass of wine and sit back on the sofa. This time, she turn on the television and watch some show that is on. She had not seen it before, which was probably because most of the time she is at work during this time of the day. It was a pretty, good show. It was kind of funny. Well at least to her. While she is sitting here, she begins to think that she had not heard from Tim today.

She calls him, and the phone goes to voicemail after about five rings. This is not like him not answering his phone, so she called back and he answered on the first ring, and said, "Babe I'm so sorry, I didn't answer the first time you called. I was in the shower, and my phone was in the bedroom. Itried to get out but by the time, I got to the phone it stopped ringing. Just as I was about to call you back, you called again, anyways, what's up, love?"

"Well I had not heard from you all morning, so I was just touching base with you.Just making sure things were all good." she says.

"I was giving you your space, sweetie. You said you and your girl were going to be having girl time. I was just respecting that." He says.

"Oh my, babe. I did not mean donot call and everything like you usually do. I was just saying that Kera will be here and Ijust wanted you to give us a little time to catch up. She is not here yet. She should be here in the airport in about an hour. Her plane is due to land here at noon." She tells him.

"Oh, okay, babe. That is cool. Well, how about you come over for a quickie and thenyou can leave from here to go pick her up?" He asked.

"Well I'm done cleaning up here so I will be right over. Just need to put the clothesin the dryer, and another load into the wash. I will be on my way to your room."

"All right, baby. That sounds great. I do not know how long Kera is visiting but I'mnot going to bother you too much. I know it has been a while since you saw each other."He explains.

"Okay, babe. I will see you in a few minutes." She tells him. She hangs up, and goes and does what she said she was and gets to Tim's. She walks in because the door is open, and he is laying on the sofa with the can of whipped cream and strawberries in his hand. He quickly jumps up and grabs her by the ass and pulls her closer. He takes off her top and lays her on the sofa and sprays a little bit cream on my chest, and licks it off.

He then takes one hand and unfastened her bra and dropped it onto the floor as he adds some cream to my left breast, and slowly licks off the cream while grabbing a strawberry and rubbing it over her lips. Julissa simply start to moan as he sucks her breast and feeds her the strawberry. It feels so good. She moaned louder. He then pulls off her shorts and panties and begins finger her inside, ashe grabs another strawberry and feeds it to her once again. They are so cold and fresh and tasted delicious, she can't control herself and what she's feeling.

She is sure it was pleasure he was giving her but that strawberry was so good. He then takes out his finger and proceeds to take her belly button and slowly move to her vagina. He licked it just right. Julissa's body starts to twinge at every single lick. She feel so good that she quickly comes and he then wants more of her, so he then picks her up and her ass is facing him. She all of a sudden feel pushing inside from behind her. Hisstrokes are so strong. I look up at the clock on his wall and see it is getting closer totime for her to go.

He continues to push in and out until he starts to feel himself about to finish. He starts to grab her ass with more passion, so she knows what is coming. She just moves with him until he moans deeper and moves much faster, then right after that he pulls out and slaps her on the ass and says, "Damn, baby! You are good to the last drop. You need to go on and get to the airport. Thanks for coming."

"I know. I really do." She says.

"Just take a quick shower, because I know you don't want to go smelling like sex.Your clothes are not wet so they will be fine to put back on." He says.

She goes and takes a quick shower and gets on out, and tries toget into her clothes so she can leave. He kept grabbing her breast and trying to seduce her once more. She finally got her clothes back on and kissed him goodbye and she's out the door. She goesto her room, grabs her bag and keys and go on to the airport.

She went for her ass to the airport because now she is a little behind her schedule, she hadto sit for herself. Julissa gets there and cure is playing here, but she is nowhere in sight. She quickly gets a call from her and she says something happened with the plane before they boarded it, and everyone had to wait for the next plane going out.She will see me in about an hour. She did not want to go back home so she figured she would just wait around for the plane to come in. She went and grabbed a bite to eat because an hour was a long time to have to wait, and as she was walking back to her seat from a distance, she saw the bitch grinning her ass off! Julissa start shaking her head as she walk towards her, and she cannot stop laughing at the look on her face. Julissa gets in her face.

And she says, "You bitch! You have me thinking I was going to be here waiting on yourass a whole hour, and you are already here! I should have known better. You play too damn much." She hugs her so tight, and tells her how much she's missed her andshe says the same. It had been a little over a month since she left me.

Well, we then walked towards the exit where she was parked and got in andtook off on the way to the suite. She turned up the music and the first thing she asked was where are the drinks?

She tells her, "I'm not drinking and driving. There are plenty of things to drink at thesuite. We can drink as soon as we get there."

"Okay, I guess I will have to just go with that. Suite?" She says.

"Yes, suite." She says.

"Oh, okay. It's money bags, high profile VP, and things!"

"Anyways, yes, you will have to go with that because first of all, you already know about these folks down here and they're driving. We need to be careful. Just last week there was a drunk driver driving recklessly and he hit this college student thatwas on our way home from school. He was all over the road and hit her from her driver side and killed her on impact. The same thing happens to my daddy and I donot want it to happen to us."

After a few more exits we reach their exit, and she turns, and they go down the street toher suite. They drive up and Dennis once again is outside dealing with this yellow girl. She quickly thinks to herself, she thought she was done with him, but she guess she loves the bad boy way he handles her, and just cannot bear to leave him alone. Kera and Julissa sit for a minute and watch as he talks all kinds of crap to her, and sheis following him like a helpless puppy needing a treat it is just sad.

Kera jumps out of the car and yells at her, and says, "Girl, he is not ever going tochange! You better get out while you can."

Dennis yells back at her, and says, "Girl, mind your own business!"

"Wow, really?" She says, "Well that is not how you treat women!"

He says, "I treat her the way I want to. You see, she has no problem with it."

"Really, Dennis. This is not how you are? I know you're not that guy." Julissa says. "Well, she just will not leave me alone. I have told her so many times that I do notwant her, but she keeps bugging me. How about you two take her off my hands?"

'No, baby, I want to stay with you." Says the yellow girl.

"Girl, aren't you like a supermodel or something?" She asked her.

She says, "Yeah. I travel all over the world, and making money is great! I meetpeople all the time."

"Okay, so why are you following behind this dude?" She asks her.

"We have been off and on now for years, and I just can't get enough of him." Sheexplains.

"You need to get over him and go find a man that treats you like a queen. He is notworth it. No man should treat any woman that way. I saw him treating you. Come on with me and my girl. We're about to go up to my sweet and have some drinks." She tellsher.

"Okay. You sure she wants me to come," as she looks at Kera.

"Oh, girl, you good. The more the merrier." Kara says.

"Can I join you all a little bit later? Dennis asks.

"No. No guys allowed!" Says Kera.

"Well, excuse me for asking!" He says.

"Oh, you are excused, and do not let it happen again." Says Kera.

"Well, the night is young, ladies." Says Julissa, "What would you like to do?"

"I want to go out!" Says Kera.

"Well that does sound like a great idea, but I just want to chill and have somedrinks." Says Julissa.

They all go inside and get in the elevator and go up to her floor.

She walks onto the door, unlocks it and shows the girls in. She says to them, "I'll beright back," and she goes a few doors down to Tim's room. She knocks on the door because this time he doesn't know she's coming, and he opens the door and says, "Hey, babe. Thought you were going to get your friend?"

"Yes, I picked her up. She is in my room with this other girl. We just metdownstairs."

"All right. Well, what are you doing here?" He asked.

"I just wanted to come and get a kiss before we start drinking, because I'm sure oncewe start I will be so trash later, I will not be coming back out until tomorrow." She says.

"Understood, so how long did you get? Can I get a little action before you go back?"He asked.

"No I got to get on back. They probably have already started without me." She says, "Oh, okay, babe. What are you all drinking?"

"I'm not sure what they started with, but I have a lot of stuff at my place now." Shesays.

She gives Tim another kiss and then gets back down the hall to her sweet. And she walks into her suite, she sees that yellow girl, and Kera taking shotswithout her. She quickly tells them that it is crazy they started without her!

They both say, "Well, you left us here alone with all this liquor. Did you honestly think we were not going to start with drinking? We figured you were busy doing something, so we just poured up some drinks, and started our own little party." Kerasays.

"Whatever, you two… just pour me a cup." She says.

They poured for me a cup of Cîroc and added some pineapple juice. Julissa drank that first drink pretty, fast and quickly got me another. The second one was a little stronger. Not sure exactly why but it was still good, so she drank it anyway. Her third she made herself, so it was not as strong. She was drinking so fast she was starting to get a little dizzy. It was feeling really hot to her so she went and changed into a little 90's silky short set.

She walk back inside and as soon as she walk in they're saying, "Why did you change?"

She says, "These drinks are hitting me pretty fast. I started to feel a little dizzy and got real, hot. I was trying to catch up with you two. Oh, well we only had about twoapiece so you fucking passed us!" Says Kera.

We all instantly started laughing until we all fell on the couch. Kera then goes toher purse and pulls out a little baggie of herb, and Julissa says, "Hey, hey, Kera, what are you doing?"

She says, "What? I'm about to get high. You know how I do, Jules!"

"Yes, but I thought you were done with that." She says.

"Yes, I was, but in New York everybody does it and then when I went to Africa, people were doing it too. I justcould not get away from it. Once I got there, a few of my friends smoked all the time, and I just decided to gethigh with them one day after lunch, and it was just something I had to have from there on out."

"Oh, I see. So all have it die hard or in this case do not really die sexually."

"Oh my gosh, Juls please do not be my mom, today! I just want to smoke my joint andenjoy time with my girl, and our new friend what's your name?" She asked.

"My name is Sharon."

"Nothing crazy. We do not have to go anywhere. We are not driving anywhere tonight. After all this just crash and sleep like a baby tonight. Is that too much toask?" Ask Kera.

"No, Kera I guess not. As long as we stay in and do not go out acting crazy tonight.I am okay with it. I might even puff a few times with you. But that is a big might!"

"Okay, now it is a party, ladies. Who wants the first puff?" Kera says.

"I will take it, Kera." Says Sharon.

"Okay now girl, puff, puff past. Do not smoke all my joints as Kera I will not smoke it all girl. I will just do a couple of puffs and pass it to Julissa." She says.

"Will, I'm about to get another drink. Do either of you want one?" asks Julissa.

"Not right now." Says Sharon.

"I will take one." Kera says.

"Okay. You sure you do not want one missy?" she asked Sharon.

"Oh, it's Sharon by the way." She explains.

"Oh, well, nice to meet you Sharon. Didn't I already ask you your name?"

"Yes, but you said 'Missy'. I was just making sure you heard me." says Kera.

"Oh, well, nice to meet you, Sharon." Says Kera in a sarcastic tone.

"Nice to meet you, too. Thank you so much for inviting me. I really needed to stopdealing with Dennis. He is a total jerk sometimes and I cannot stand that." Said Sharon.

"Well, we already knew. Dude was rude as hell to you outside earlier somebody needs to teach him a lesson and manners when dealing with women." Say Kera.

"Yes, ladies. I know but who would be willing to do something like that?" She asked.

"Oh, girl. I know plenty of people that would love to teach a womanizer a lesson." Says Kera.

"Really? That is crazy! Sharon says.

"Well, everyone is not like him sweetie.Some guys actually want the best for their woman." Says Kera and goes in to turns up the music and they begin to dance.

Julissa goes into the kitchen and grabs another glass and then fills it up with more Cîroc and takes them to the girls and they all take the shots. It was so strong. "Ohmy gosh, I could not believe, actually took it straight I am usually so chicken!"

Kera looks at Julissa like are you okay? She reassures her she is fine, and they dance around some more. Julissa goes and grabs her phone and sees that she has acall from Dennis, and quickly deletes it. She then gets a text from him that says damn I want to come see you. Why will you not let me come? She is not who I want. It is you!

Julissa texts him back and says you know why. Stop trying to make it seem likeyou are such a good guy. I have a man. Bye.

He texts back and says, well if he is such a good guy why is he not with you? Julissa texts back and says we are having a girl's night. I do not need to explain anything to you. It should be no concern of yours anyway. Do not text me back!

Kera walks over to her, and it's looking over her shoulder as she is texting the lasttext, and she says, "Dennis? Isn't that the asshole's name?"

Julissa says, "Yes, but that is not him. It's another Dennis I know."

"I guess, I believe that you better not be talking to that jerk." Says Kera.

"What are you two talking about over there?" Sharon says as she walks over where they are.

Kera says, "She over here texting some guy named Dennis."

"My Dennis?" Sharon asked.

"No, as a matter of fact it is another Dennis." Says Julissa.

"Oh, well, it better not be my Dennis, because, girl, I do not play about my man!" Says Sharon.

"It's not him, girl, so drop that little hard ass act!" Says Kera, "she said it's not him so that is that!"

"Well let me see your phone, Julissa. I can easily clear this all up. All I need to do is see the number." Sharon says.

"I am not giving you my phone! You might as well hang that shit up because it's not happening." Say Julissa.

"Well, if it's not him, why won't you show me the number?" Sharon yells across the room.

"Girl, first of all, this is my place. I do not have to show your ass anything! I told you it was not him, and you need to calm your ass down and believe that!" She yells back to her.

"Sharon you better do yourself a favor and just drop it before we send your ass back to that sorry ass nigga!" Says Kera.

"Whatever, it better not be him that is all I'm saying!" Sharon says.

"Or what, bitch? Or what? Cure ass because I know damn well you are not threatening my girl in my presence. I know she got way better taste than that anyway, so don't even!"

"You know what, I am going to leave, and go ask him myself." She says.

"And do not bring your ass back here either. She told you that it was not him so you should have just listened instead of being all suspicious and shit!" Kara tells her. She walks toward the door and Kera slams it behind her.

Kera then turns to Julissa and says, "That is that nigga, isn't it?"

She tells her, "Yes but the way he treats her, he never treated me that way. He was a total gentleman, and I never had any problems out of him till he found out what I was up to."

"Oh damn. What the hell did you do? So hold on. First, let me get this straight. You, and him dated. I am thinking maybe once they were in their relationship often? Then you fucked him over. How?"

"It is a long story, but, yes." She says.

"Well, damn, I knew it was him but, I just couldn't get past the asshole, and you being into him part. Now, I understand. He just does not want her ass! He wants you back doesn't he? So I need a little more information. What did you do to him?" asks Kera.

"I played his ass to get the VP job, but I was not planning to fall in love with him." She tells her.

"So, where does the love part come in?" Ask Kera.

"We were dating for a little while, and we had a great time. Like I said before, he was good to me. He knew I was worth it. Anyways I just got caught up in the fun and messed around and fell in love." She says.

"Okay, so what do you think he is going to tell her?" She asked.

"Hey, I do not know and nor do I care! She cannot whoop my ass! I am not worriedabout Miss Chris. I got my own relationship to worry about." She says.

"Relationship? Wait, what, with who? Oh my, damn girl. You got an episode of JerrySpringer right here in the middle of Atlanta. Okay, spill it, bitch. I need to know allthe details, especially if that girl comes back here with some shit." She says.

"Okay, remember back in the day, the guy I was with?" She asked.

"No. I do not think, I do." She says.

"Tim." She says. "Oh yeah. That dude. Okay, I'm listening." She says. "Hold on. Didn'the leave and go to the military or something like that?" she asked.

"Yes, anyways, he came back to town to find me. We went on a date, one thing lead to another and we decided to try it again. He has done so much with his life. The military really shipped him into shape. He is more mature now and he knows whatthe future holds.

"Okay, so he came back here looking for you, but what about Mr. Loverboy? When did you two get together and how long was it? Because I am not the wisest person,but I bet he was dating that girl at the same time. Damn girl. I am writing Jerry a letter now. He needs to hear this shit!" Says Kera.

"You better not write them. You know that show can get really out of hand sometimes. I do not need that crazy Sharon coming after me and getting her ass whooped on national TV because if she comes after me, I'm going to throw up! Iwill have to go back to my ghetto days! That was when I did not care about anything people had to say about me. I just did me! Now, I have an image to hold.My boss hates drama. I really do not need that in my life. I want to keep my job,and I would lose it for sure if I got into a televised fight with that damn girl!"

"Anyways, girl, it's still early. You still want to go out?" Ask Kera.

"No, I'm good. Would be our luck, old Sharon ass will show up, and I'd have to throw these hands anyway!"

"Okay, so what do you want to do?" Ask Kera.

"I don't know." Julissa says she walks toward the stereo and turns it up, and begins todance. Kera joins her after taking a sip of her drink.

"Remember when we were in college, and we used to always get into trouble becauseof how loud our music was?" Ask Julissa.

"Yeah we had some loud ass music." says Kera.

"Of course. I used to be the one to turn it up as high as it would go, and have all thepeople down the hall singing and dancing. Those were some fun times," says Kera. As they both kept dancing. The music wasn't quite as high but it was pretty loud.

The people next door started banging on the walland yelling for them to turn the music down!

Julissa quickly went and turned it down. The next song that came on was somelove song.

"Don't start looking all weird in the face."

86

"So what was the deal with you and Mr. Michaels?" Ask Kera.

"He was all in love andstuff and I messed it up!" To listen then quickly sums up sums up to cure.

"What? That sounds crazy. How did you do that? By the way he is hella fine." SaysKera.

"Well my job wanted to sign him, but they couldn't get his attention, so I was offered a VP position to sign him by any means necessary, and I did but in themeantime dating him it really feels like I really feel for him." Julissa says sadly.

"Oh, boo, well maybe y'all can talk again?" Says Kera.

"Oh, no. Hell no. He said some things he can't take back, and plus I am now with Tim.I wouldn't do that to him. Dennis had some good luck dick, but he honestly wasreally boring at times." She says, "But thank you to herself damn I miss him!"

"Oh, okay then I guess," says Kera.

"What if you don't believe me?" Says Julissa.

"Well, me knowing you and your past with guys it tells me that you loved this dude,and must still be in love with him. Mr. Michaels it is," says Kera.

"Oh, you don't know what you're talking about but you can think whatever you want.I am so over him! He is such an asshole, and I can't believe how he treated me when it was all said and done." As a tear drops from her left eye. She turns her cheek just in, Kera goes to her, and hugs her and tells her she needs to stop fighting, and face her true feelings, at least to get over him.

"I'm trying so hard to get my mind off of him, but he is just he just keeps showing up. How can I get him out of my mind and hard when he's always around? I reallylike Tim, but he is innocent in all of this." Says Julissa.

"Well I suggest you tell Dennis to completely leave you alone!" Said Kera.

"I can't exactly do that when I work with the man. Although I could seriously avoidhim as much as I can. I want him and I know he wants me too." Says Julissa.

"Okay, then, my love, you need to figure out a way to make that happen, and for him to go away. At least to give you some time." Says Kera.

"I'm going to have a talk with my boss and see if there is something going on thatwe can send him to. If not then I'll just have to be strong, and not go for his advances. We were so good together, why did I have to ruin it?"

"Well, I suggest you stop thinking about him. Get your mind off of him. And it's getting late so we should probably go to sleep. I'm getting tired of hearing your softstories of Mr. Finest Wine and Mr. Michaels too much. You're putting a dread on my hanging out and enjoying ourselves part." says Kera.

"Oh yeah. You keep talking about this nigga like the sex was so good, and you missing him and stuff. I am single. It's annoying. Let's try to enjoy ourselves please? Cuz I miss my girl. Don't want no drama."

"All right, Missy. I'll go get us some more drinks and the next time you are talking crazy we going to have a problem!" Says Julissa, "cuz you were so mean to me!"

"I'm sorry, love, but it was too much. The girl coming over here, and all these shenanigans with you and your ex. Let's just drink and turn up. I'm glad we didn'tgo out." Says Kera.

"Yeah, me too, but it was so crazy seeing Dennis. Looking all fine, and stuff withthat girl, what was her name again." Asked Julissa.

"It was Sharon, you're jealous, stopped acting like you forgot that name already. She was so out of line, and if she brings that back, I'm kicking her ass myself!" SaysKera all rolled up.

"Damn, there you go again."

"Got me all lit over here." Says Kera.

"Okay, okay, no more talk of either of them. I'm over it." Says Julissa.

"Let's take a shot. What else you got in there?" Asked Kera.

"Oh, I have some tequila thatTim brought the other day. I'll find some shot glasses and we need to take a shot!"

"I'm down for that," says Kera.

"Yes I thought he brought some. Here it is," Julissa says while looking in the fridge.

"Will stop talking so much and open the bottle. I am ready to have some fun." SaysKera looking all anxious.

"Okay, okay," she pours two shots, then gives one to herself and the other to care. "What are we toasting to? Sheasked.

"How about, great friends that would do anything for the other?"

"Okay!" Says Julissa.

"To great friends!" As they pick up their glasses and tapped them together and atthe same time put them to their mouths, and quickly swallow.

"Oh, my it's like midnight. Don't you have something with your mom tomorrow?" asksKera.

"Yes, but you're coming too, right? You said you wanted to see her before you left?" Says Julissa.

"Oh yes, I have to see Mama Lucky before I have to go back, and your brother is going to come too right and bring some girl he has been seeing? I can't wait to seehim though. It's been quite a while since I saw him. Of course Mama was lucky too, okay let's go to bed. I've talked enough." says Kera.

"Why are you trying to see my brother so badly?"

"No reason. It's just been a long timesince I saw him is all!" Says Kera.

"Seriously? You don't still have that crush on him do you?" Asks Julissa.

"No, girl. I don't. I never did. He was like my brother we just were cool with each other." Says Kera.

"All right, whatever, let's go to sleep! I'm tired," says Julissa.

"Me too," as they both fallasleep on the couch.

"Good night, girl, love you Glad you came to visit." Says Julissa.

"Yeah, yeah, yeah. Yada, Yada, Yada go to sleep. Love you too." says Kera.

Both of them turn their backs to each other thinking about old times. Julissa of course was thinking about Dennis, and Kera about Alex as they both start fallingasleep and soon are knocked out.

Chapter 12

Dinner at Mama Lucky's

It is about 7:30 A.M. in the morning, and Julissa wakes up because she has to use the restroom. She quietly gets up, and hurries to the bathroom. Once she was in there she decided to take a quick shower because looking at the clock before she came in she could see that it was not going to be very long before she had to go seeher mom. Kera can't leave without seeing her. She thought.

Once she gets out of the shower, her phone rings, and it wakes Kera up. She quickly grabs the phone and brings it to Julissa. She then says (while walkingtowards Julissa) "It's Tim"

Julissa grabs the phone, and says "Hey babe. What's up?"

"I was just calling to see if you are still going to your moms." He asks "Or did youwant to do something with your man tonight?"

"Awe, sorry, babe, but yes. Kera and I are going to mom's for dinner with my brother, and his new girlfriend, and her twin daughter. Gonna be a long afternoon/night. My brother usually doesn't date anyone with kids." Julissa explains.

'Would you like me to come to your mom's?" He asks.

"No, babe. It's already going to be a lot of people there. I don't want to overwhelmMom too much! I am sure she would love to see you, but how about we do something next week with her?" She suggests.

"Okay, that sounds good. Well, my boy wanted me to work at the club tonightanyways. Now, I'll just tell him I'll work tonight." He says.

"The club, wow! Why didn't you just lead with that?" Says Julissa.

"Oh, baby don't get all out of shape. It's just to help with my new venture with myboy and make a little change. Nothing to worry about, my love." He says.

"Yeah, haha. Okay, you better be glad I'm going to be busy. We might hit up the clubafter anyways." She says

"So, babe. It would be great to see you walk through that door. Kera can cometoo." Tim says.

"All right, so I guess you don't have anything else to do today?" She asks.

"I'm going to see if Kera wants to go to the gym, and get in a great workout for a bitthis morning, then maybe go and grab some lunch. Once we are done, I will call you to meet us wherever we decide to go and eat." Says Julissa.

"Okay, babe. That sounds great. You want me to eat lunch with you today?" Heasks again to make sure.

"Yes, my love. You need to meet Kera, and talk a bit."

"I can't wait." He says.

"Well, I am gonna call you in a 'lil while." She says.

"Okay, bye now." Tim says and hangs up.

As she gets off the phone Kera walks in talking about "I heard you say somethingabout the gym. Well, sis, you know I am always down for workout! Also always down to go and see some sexy gray sweats, and shorts. All sweaty and things. Oh,my I am getting overheated over here just thinking about it." She says.

"I am gonna jump in the shower, and get dressed and then we can go." Says Kera.

"Alright, girl. With you crazy ass! I knew you would certainly be down for that.Okay. Go and get yourself together. Time is ticking, and go!" Julissa says joking.

'I'm going. I'm going!" Says Kera as she goes to get ready.

Julissa's phone rings again, and this time it is Mama Lucky. "boo bear, when youcome can you please bring some juice? I have everything else here to drink." Shesays, "I am not sure what those girls would like to drink."

"No problem, mom. I will pick up some on my way there, later."

"Oh yeah, and also some rolls. Try to come a little early so I can throw them in theoven before everyone shows up." She says.

"Well, we will see you all later. About to go to the gym." Says Julissa.

"Oh yeah, boo bear, Kera's coming tonight, too, right?" Asks Mama Lucky.

"Yes, ma. She will be with me." Says Julissa.

"Alright, now. We are going to have a great time! I'm going to have a house full, butfull of family so it's okay. Please don't forget the juice and roll sweetie." Mama Lucky says.

"Also, will Tim be here? Because you know Lester is coming too. Family is what Ilive for!"

"Okay, Mom, I got you. I will see what he says. He might be busy. We will see youlater." Says Julissa.

"Hey, Mama Lucky." Kera yells into the phone as she walks in. "Can't wait to tasteyour cooking again. Oh and to see you too." She says.

"You better have changed that all right, baby girl. See y'all tonight. Love you. Bye."

"Love you too, Mama Lucky and miss you."

"Bye, Mom," as Julissa hangs up, she startslaughing. "We need to go!" Says Julissa.

"Okay, I just need to put this hair in a ponytail and put on my sneakers." Says Kera, "then we can go."

"Oh girl, I love that workout suit. You are prepared at all times aren't you? Trying toget all the attention," says Julissa.

"Shit I better with all this voluptuousness harvest we're sitting up all perfect and thatfit was on point, I'm looking for a man, I would stay a little longer, if I didn't need to get back to work. Them African dudes are just not for me, but these ATL niggas are just my type." Says Kera.

"Girl, let's go. It is almost 9:00 A.M, and we have to get in for at least an hour. Then we'llcome back here, and shower and change for lunch with Tim." Says Julissa.

"Okay, so I get to meet Mr. Wonderful?" She asked.

"Yes, he suggested lunch since I won't really see him until late tonight."

"Oh yeah, boo,I did hear you mentioned we're going out later after Mama Lucky's." Says Kera.

"Yes, I think we could use a night out." Send Julissa, "No drugs this time."

"ATL ain't ready for this jelly." Says Kera as she shakes her booty, and startstwerking.

"Okay, enough of all that, let's go!" As they begin to walk out the door, Kera's phonerings.

She quickly puts it on do not disturb and doesn't talk about it anymore, looking atbig day she puts it in her side pocket of her shorts.

"Who is that?" Asked Julissa.

"Nobody, please don't worry about it." Says Kera.

They left their suite, and Headed downstairs to the gym. It is quite packed. Thereare a lot of people. Hardly any machines left to work on.

After a few minutes of walking around we finally see two ladies on the treadmillsget off, and wipe down their machines, then look our way, in motion over for us tocome and grab the machines before anyone else can.

We get on the treadmills and begin to walk for a little while. We then begin a light job. That walk was not feeling like a good workout. The job felt better. We actually started sweating a little bit. Normally Julissa did not sweat, but she was drenched. They both start looking around to see where they are going next. Julissa spotted one machine in the corner, so they decided to get off the treadmill, and go to the open machine intake terms. It is the legs machine. You set up what weight you want, and then put your legs inside, and push your guys in and outward. Julissa did about20 reps then Kera got on. As she was doing her reps, and another person gets off ofanother machine. It was not the same machines so they just stayed on that machine.Each did one more set of 20. After that they went to the squat machines that were open now. There were a lot of people who left. After about two sets of each, they were both covered in sweat.

"Damn, you ladies came here for a real real workout." Said some guy.

Kera quickly has to come with a reply. "Yes and so what are you trying to say? Wedid that right, Lisa." Says Kera.

"Yes, indeed I am tired. Ready for a shower," says Julissa.

"I hope you ladies come back again. It was very nice watching you work out. Neversaw women really working it out quite like you two," says the guy.

"Whatever, you better be glad you're sexy or I would have just walked away."

"You are so full of it, but yes we get it in. Yes, we come to see the guys, and be nosywatching the fake women that come in here trying to act like they are doing something." Kera says with a big grand and started to laugh.

"Can I have your number, Ms. Feisty? I want to see why you are so feisty." Says theguy.

"First of all, what is your name?" Asks Julissa.

"Oh, my bad. Sorry for not using my manners. I am Adrian. Adrian Austin." As hegrabs a business card out of a little pouch on his side. "I am the owner of Delta Insurance, here in Atlanta, but we have several other spots in the world. Cali, Florida, New Mexico. Anyways enough about me. Your question?"

"Mrs.?" He asked.

"Julissa is her name, and I am Kera. She lives here, but I am here visiting." Says Kera.

"Well it was a pleasure to meet you such beautiful queens. Well, Julissa, if youlive here I wonder why I've never seen you before now. I come to the gym regularly."

"She's not interested, man, she got a man!" Snapped Kera.

"Not to be a smart-ass or anything, Miss Kera, but can we let Miss Julissa speak?" Says Adrian.

"She's right, I do have a boyfriend. Tell us a confirmation and we areactually needing to go. Nice meeting you. Bye."

"Yes, the pleasure was all mine!" Says Adrian as he walks down the hall.

"Girl, why do you do that? No, I was not going to talk to him, but that was some crazy stuff. That's not like you. Kera, does this attitude have something to do withthat call earlier?" Asks Julissa.

"No and I said not to bother me about that." Just as Julissa was about to saysomething, a curious phone rang.

Again Kara tries to hide it, but Julissa caught a glimpse of the name before shecould completely cover the screen.

"Kera, who is that?" Asks Julissa.

"Nobody! And that's all." Yells Kera.

"Oh, hell no. You are not going to not answer a phone call. Start acting all in unfamiliar, and then when I ask you, yell at me! I know this person must have scared you because you've been acting differently since that first call. Now tell me who he is. I need you to be yourself again!"

"Okay, okay, damn, sis. You'renot going to leave this alone are you?"

"No, I'm not." Says Julissa.

"It was a guy that I once talked to here in Atlanta. He must know I'm in town because he won't stop bothering me. Anyways when we were younger. He would always come, and hang with my brother. Will this actually happen before they were friends? He raped me in the basement after we had dated for a little while. One dayhe came to the house while my mom and dad were not there, and he tried to have sex and I was not having it, and so he ripped my shorts off of me and had his friend hold me down, while he did it to me!"

"Oh my god. That is why you are avoiding that creep, I'm glad you told me, but I can't believe that happened to you, sis. Who is this guy and why didn't you tell anyone?"

"Julissa, he swore if I told anyone, he would kill me!"

"Kill you, OMG. The nerve of this asshole. I will call my cousins now. They will find his ass and makehim disappear. We don't need to have you so scared. He needs to pay! Do you remember their friend?"

"No, but he kept calling him Debo. That's all I remember,"

"And this do not answercall, who is he?" Julissa asks

"Lisa. I don't want them to get into trouble. This dude knows a lot of people. They could be friends with him, and then I get to worry even more." Kera is scared.

"Well, tell me his name, and I'll do a little research. Can find himself, and see who he knows and knows him. My cousins don't like that shit. Especially, the way they didit!"

"I wish he would just leave me alone! I can't say I forgot about it, but I was trying to leave it in the past." Says Kera.

"Oh no. No, no, no, past my ass. We are going to make sure he doesn't do that to anyone else! He should get what's coming to him! I don't want to make any trouble."Says Kera.

"Oh, don't worry, you won't be involved at all. Who is he?" Asks Julissa again.

"His name is Mac. Or at least that's what people called him."

"Mac? Oh, hell no."

"I know him. He was friends with my brother until he got into drugs. He's been in jail so many times. He is probably in there now. Don't worry I'll find out. Says Julissa.

"Okay, Julissa. Thank you." Says Kera.

"You know I got your back no matter what."

"Well enough of this talk about old stuff. We need to go and shower and get dressed for lunch." Says Kera as they walked to the elevators and up to the suite,and literally race to the bedroom. Laughing like crazy, and instantly stop as Julissa grabs Kera and hugs her sotight, and says, "I'm gonna make sure he pays just to listen

Okay." As she hugs her back and starts to cry Julissa holds her tighter, and they cry together.

Kera moves away and runs to the shower, before she does that she says she needs to go to the bathroom. All Julissa hears next is the shower running.

"Really, Kera." Julissa says, "That's not what you said you were going to do. We were having a moment, but I'll let you have it. Just hurry up 'cuz it's almost 11:00, and weboth need to get in there."

Julissa turns on the TV. Because she couldn't exactly get in the shower yet. So shedecides to watch TV. After about 20 more minutes, when Kera finally gets out. Julissa had fallen asleepwatching TV.

She yells out to her that she is done, then Julissa wakes up from her little nap and says,'Damn, sis. It's about time! I fell asleep over here waiting on you."

"Well, we sweated a lot today so I had to be smelling good."

"Whatever," as she turns on her music on the phone and then gets in the shower. Kera goes into her suitcases and finds a cute little dress to put on since the weather was niceout today, and then sit on the couch.

Julissa took about a 15-minute shower, and get on out, because she knew theyneeded to go pretty soon. She also finds a cute little dress. Spaghetti straps. Showing all her cleavage and so snug.

"Ooh. Sexy mama." Says Kera as she walks into the bedroom.

'You look great yourself."

"I'm ready when you are, love." Says Kera.

"I think I'm going to grab a little jacket incase it rains. Talk about Georgia weather." Julissa goes to the bedroom, and comes back out with a jacket, and they both get on the elevator and go downstairs to the car.

They get in and drive to the spot where they were eating. It was called Holman andFinch.

"Kera, here can you send to my message and tell him to meet us at Holman and Finch"

"Okay, done, sis." Kera says.

"What did he say?" Asks Julissa.

"He said, okay, no problem. See y'all there." Kera reads Tim's message out loud.

They arrived at the restaurant. Both get out and start to walk in just as Tim isdriving up. He goes to Julissa with the big hug and a kiss on the cheek.

Kera pretends to dab him and he then says, "Oh, we are funny?"Even hugs her, but nothing more.

"Hi, I'm Tim. I'm sure you are Kera. Well, I have heard a lot about you."

"About me?Julissa I hope you haven't told any of my secrets."

"Oh, no, she didn't." Says Tim. "All good things! She told me how you are such a badassin Africa."

"Okay. Okay, did she? Well it's nice to finally meet you. She has told me nothingabout you," says Kera with a smirk on her face.

"Anyways, you two, I'm hungry. I hope we have a table. If not, we can sit a fewminutes and wait for one to open up."

"It usually is not too long." Says Julissa as she walks up to the counter. She says, "A table for three for luck."

"Oh, yes, Ms. Lucky, right this way. I saved you a table," saysthe waitress with the name tag that says her name was Kamara.

She seats them and hands them all menus. "I've never been here, babe, what do theyhave or is it a variety?" Asks Tim.

"Yes, babe, you just look at the menu." She says.

"All I want is a big juicy, steak andsome potatoes or something." Kera says.

"Well, I'm sure there are some steaks on the menu." Says Julissa.

"Yes. It is a skillet beefsteak for $30and comes with rice cooked chips in Paris butter."

"Paris butter? What? Julissa asks.

"Bougie ass place you got us at?" Yells Kera.

"Keep your voice down. The food is reallygood." She says.

"I think I'm going to order the roasted chicken. How about you, Tim?" Asks Julissa.

"I thinkI'll have steak too. Good choice, Kera." He says.

The waitress comes back to the table to get their drink order but they all go ahead and order their food.

It only takes her a few minutes to bring out their drinks. Tim just wanted water for now, but orders a bottle of wine for the table. She brings water back for everyone, anyway. The waitress opens the bottle for them and they all grab their glasses and she pours. Another waitress then brings them some rolls with butter for the table in case they wanted something to snack on, and leaves it. They all sit and talk for a little while, basically getting to know each other. Then they drink their wine until the food shows up. Kera has had a few glasses too many and all she can do is laugh.

"Stop that!" Julissa says, "You know you can't drink."

"I'm okay, Lisa, really." Says Kera.

"Okay, well, then calm down. Nothing is that funny," says Julissa in a smart ass tone.

"My bad, love. I'm sorry." Says Kera.

"It's okay, but we are in this place, down, please!"

A few minutes later the food arrives. They converse a little more while eating. Kera eats her steak and potatoes with her salad. Julissa eats her chicken, but said her veggies were too hard and that she didn't really like them. While Tim eats little of his steak and mac and cheese and asks for a to-go box for the leftovers because he had eaten too much bread.

"I have to go to the ladies' room. I think I'm about to throw up!" Says Kera.

"Okay, I'll go with you to help." Says Julissa.

"Well, I'll go pay the check, and we can go." says Tim.

"Okay, babe. We will be right back. She just needs to throw up, and then she should feel a little better." Says Julissa.

"All right, go," he says, "she needs you."

"Well, don't leave." She says.

"I'm not." Says Tim as he walks toward the counter.

Julissa hurries to the bathroom where Cara is puking her guts out, and grabs her hair.

"You drink that wine way too fast that's why you feel like crap. Even in college you didn't do well with wine. Remember freshman year at Georgia State, that party we went to. You didn't want any liquor, so you drank wine instead and we both know what happened that night."

"Oh my gosh. You didn't, we vowed to never speak of that night again. I was torn up, anyways."

"Well, at least, this time I'm here with you." Says Julissa. "I'm done, won't speak of it ever again. My bad, we did say that! Let's get you cleaned up. You must have really made it."

"Yeah, it was coming once I came through the door. I couldn't stop it." Cara says.

"It's even on your dress." Says Julissa. "No more wine for you! I know Mom will have some too, and you need not drink any, especially, 'cuz we will be going out after and I don't need this happening again."

"Yeah, whatever," says Kera. "I'll be sober by tonight. Maybe, we just need to go and chill until later."

Once again, Kera's phone rings, and it's that guy that they do not want to answer or do anything with again. Her phonewas on the floor so Julissa picks it up and answers with, "Who is this? Kera can't come to the phone right now." And immediately the person on the phone just hangs up!

Kera says, "What happened?"

"Nothing, but dude better be in jail 'cuz he just hung up in my face. Rude ass. I'mcalling my cousin now."

Julissa grabs her phone, and calls her cousin Curtis known as trouble. He answers on the first ring.

"What's up cuz. I need a favor." Says Julissa.

"Okay, what you need? And do I haveto take somebody's ass?"

"Well, my girl got raped by Mack."

"Oh, who you say?"

"Mack, cuz."

"Great? Oh, we don't do women being disrespected, especially, my people."

"Yeah, cuz. It happened a long time ago. But he keeps calling her, and she is scaredto death."

"Oh, Mack in the pen. He's been doing the same thing for 30 years. He did it to someunderage girl, and she yelled rape, and they put his ass straight in jail, no parole!"

"Okay, so what do you want from me, cuz?"

"Make him pay, cuz. My girl wants him to pay." Says Julissa.

"All right, cuz, I'm a bit busy. I got boys in there that can make that happen. She will neverget another call after they take care of him."

"Thanks, cuz!" Says Julissa.

"And, cuz, we never spoke, right?" He asked.

"No, cuz, peace." And hangs up. After a bit Kera and Julissa walk out of the bathroom.

"What the hell were y'all doing in there?" Tim asked.

"Oh, she had thrown up all over the place. It was only right to cleanup." Says Julissa.

"Let's go, girl. I want to be able to rest up a while till dinner tonight." Says Kera.

Timhugs Julissa and kisses her softly and says, "Goodbye, ladies. Kera, it was nice meeting you. I will see you all later, right, babe?" as he looks at Julissa.

"Yes, after dinner, we are going to come out for drinks." Says Julissa. They get into thecar, and drive back to the suite, and go upstairs. As they are walking into the suite. Julissa remembers that she needed to go to the store for her mom. She then says, "I got to go to the store. Mom wants me to bring some stuff."

"Okay, well, I'm going to take a shower for the third time today, and take a nap. I'll see you when you get back." Says Kera.

"Sure thing, love. I won't be very long. The store isn't far."

Julissa goes to the store pretty quick and comes back with the juice and rolls. She puts the juice in the fridge and the rolls on the counter and goes to lay down in herbed. She thought it's been a long ass morning and she needed to take a moment to relax.

They both ended up sleeping so well even if it was only for a little while, when Julissa's cell rings, and she picks her phone up to see that it is her mama.

"Boo bear, I hope you got that stuff, and are on your way over here. I need to warmup those roles before everyone gets here." Says mama Lucky.

"All right, Mom. What time is it?"

"It is 5:30."

"Oh no, Mom. Not on our way yet, but it won't be long we will be. See you soon."

"Okay, hurry up," says mama Lucky.

Julissa and Kera get up and get themselves together, and out the door quickly. As they almost get to the elevator, Julissa realizes she forgot the items to bring. She goes back while Kera waits at the elevator, and then they go on together and head tomama Lucky's.

They arrive, and see Alex outside on the porch, pacing as if he is nervous orsomething.

"Damn, bro, what's the matter?" Asked Julissa.

"What promises? Do you think she will say yes?" He asked as he showed her theengagement ring.

"Really, wow. You trying to be all tied up?" Asked Julissa.

"Yes, sis. She is the one!" Alex said.

"Oh yeah you said that! I'm happy for you, bro. Let's goinside I want to see Mama Lucky," says Kera as she starts walking towards the house.

They all go inside. Tanae and her girls are sitting on the couch in the living roomwatching TV.

Mama Lucky is in the kitchen, and Kera goes straight to her, and hugs her extra tight. Kisses her on her cheek. Julissa then comes in and hugs her too. Alex comesin, shows her the ring, and she screams, "Oh my gosh, really?"

"Yes, Mom." Says Alex.

"All I need to do is warm the roast and we can eat, everyone. Boo bear, where are therolls?" she asked.

"Oh my bad, they're in the car." Says Alyssa.

Melissa jumps up and goes out to the car to grab the bag, and gets back in asquickly as possible. Mama Lucky grabs the bag, takes the rolls out before opening the bag and quickly putsthem in the pan. While they are warming up, everyone goes into the living room.All of a sudden, Alex grabs Tanae by the hand.

"Honestly, I never knew what love was before I met you. I enjoy your company. Yourgirls are amazing, and I want you all to be in my life forever. Baby, I love you and these girls and I just want to ask you…" as he pulls the ring out of his pocket.

"Tanae Denise Anderson, will you marry me?" As he spoke a tear dropped from his eye.

She hugs him and says, "Yes, yes, I would love to marry you."

He then says, "I know we haven't known each other long, but I'm looking forward to learning more about you and these sweet girls." As he hugs them too.

Mama Lucky says, "Well, congratulations to you two. You seem like a good woman for my son. I wish your dad could have been here to see this big day for you too."

"Congrats, bro, and my soon to be sis-in-law," said Julissa

"Congrats, congrats to y'all." Says Kera.

"All right, it's time to eat!" Says mama Lucky.

"Mr. Alex, you going to make my mom so happy," says the twins, and they hug him and Tanae both.

Everyone then goes to the kitchen to grab their food.

"I'm not fixing nobody food, so y'all need to grab a plate off the counter, and the fork or spoon then make you, your own plate. I don't know what y'all eat." Says mama Lucky.

"Okay, Mama we got it." Julissa says.

"Girls, do what she said," says Tanae.

"Okay, Mom," says the twins as they both grabbed a plate, and picked the foods they wanted, and sat in the family room. Everyone got their food, and drinks and they went to the table.

"Alex say Grace, please, son," says mama Lucky.

"Okay, Mom." Everyone bows your heads. He says the grace and everyone replies with a unanimous Amen. Dinner was pretty quick. The table was quiet because nobody was talking as everyone was busy eating. Dinner was done, and all of them settled in the living room watching some movie, it was like 8:00 P.M.

"Well, Mom, thanks for dinner, and bro congratulations on your engagement, but Kera and I will be going now. Y'all have a good rest of your night, but we have plans," says Julissa.

"Oh, so that is what we do now? Come, eat, and then leave immediately after? Oh no little lady. You're going to help me clean up the kitchen, and then y'all can leave." Says mama Lucky.

"Okay, Mama Lucky, we will help!" Says Kera.

"Mom, come on. We need to go!" Says Julissa

"Girl, come on. It won't take that long! She cooked. The least we can do is help clean," says Kera.

They then help mama Lucky clean up the kitchen, and head to the car once they are done and have said their goodbyes. As they reach the car, mama Lucky yells. "Y'all don't want to take any plates with you?"

"No, Mom. We are okay but thanks," As they get in the car.

"My girls. Kera, it was so good to see you. Love you." She says.

"You too, mama Lucky. Love you, too, bye."

They drive off towards the suite. Go on upstairs and chill, and watch some TV. Thinking about Tim and the club. Neither one of them really want to go now. Theyare full and relaxed.

Tim calls and says, "You are also coming out tonight right?"

"I don't know, babe. We are full, and just relaxing. Plus Kera don't need no more todrink," says Julissa.

"Seriously, babe?" Says Tim.

"Yes. But when you get home you can call me. We are staying in tonight."

"Okay, I can understand that. It's going to be late. You will probably sleep." Says Tim.

"Maybe, but you can still try," says Julissa.

"Okay, babe. I'll call you later. I have to be there by 9:30 to open the doors."

"All right, babe. I'll talk to you later," says Julissa.

"Okay, bye."

They relaxed a little bit more watching something on Netflix, they were interested in, and eventually, fell asleep!

Some hours later, Julissa wakes up with Tim calling to say goodnight.

"Okay, babe. Goodnight. See you tomorrow." She says while walking to her bedroom. She then grabs a blanket from the closet and lays it over Kera, then returns to her bed,and instantly falls back asleep.

Chapter 13

Bad News & Good News

Waking up to the bright sun shining through her window Julissa gets up, and goes to the restroom. Grabbed her phone on the way, and started flipping through her social media. While flipping, she saw that Dennis was out with a new lady. At first,she thought she knew who it was, but then she realized she didn't. Thinking, he messing with everyone now. Such a hoe!

She keeps scrolling, and sees Jen. She's all posted up with the guy she metat the club that night they went out. Good for her, she thought! She looks so happy.I need to call her, but maybe I'll ask her to go to lunch tomorrow. She thought.

"Let me get up and out of here. I need to go into a quick meeting with my boss, and thenI will be back to pick you up to take you to the airport." She says to Kera, who had also woken up along with Julissa.

"Oh, don't worry about me. I'm staying another night. If that's okay with you?" Says Kera "Remember the guy I was seeing here I told you about once I arrived here?" Asked Kera.

"Yes, but I didn't think it was anything serious." Says Julissa.

"Well, actually we've been talking to each other since our fun night that i told youabout." Says Kera "He's actually pretty sweet. He's just been away working, and he just landed here last night. I have plans to go see him today. We are kinda spending the day together."

"What do you mean, 'kinda'?" Asked Julissa "So, let me get this straight. Youcanceled your flight home, to hook up with some guy you just met? Your miss-workaholic ass is going to miss work due to some, I guess, good sex?"

"Yes, that about sums it up!" Says Kera.

"So, have you called your people back home yet?" Asked Julissa.

"Yes, yes, and yes bitch! Why are you so worried about what I'm doing?" Kera asksin quite a loud tone.

"Well, for one thing, you are staying here. When is your flight for tomorrow?"

Julissa asks.

"Of course, I am. I wouldn't have stayed anywhere else. You are my girl. I mean,you are actually being a little judgmental right now, but you are still my girl. Toanswer the second question. My flight will depart at 10 A.M. Is there anything elsethat you would like to know?" She asked.

"Well, since you are trying to have a whole attitude over there. I don't need to knowanything else. Just to tell you to be careful. If something doesn't sit right with you Ineed you to get out ASAP!" Says Julissa.

"Okay, mom. I will be careful." She says with a slight grin.

"So, you're telling me also that you will be spending the night with him?" She asked"Pretty much, but I will be here in time for my ride with you to the airport, unless you've changed your mind."

Says Kera

"Yes, I am still taking you." Says Julissa

"Can we leave by 8:30 because I want to make sure I get there early because I needto get a little work done." Asked Kera I will have to go to work as soon as I get offthe plane."

"I'm sure it won't be an issue for me tomorrow instead of today. Mr. Prince can do without me for our morning briefing. I will be back in time for the afternoon. Okay,boo. Please, be careful and keep your location on just in case I need to find you. So,you're leaving when?"

"I don't know exactly yet." Says Kera.

"So whatever. It doesn't matter. I still need to shower, and get dressed for this quickmeeting on our updates for the week." Says Julissa.

"Okay, well, I'm going to make a pot of coffee. I don't drink it, but today I feel kindof tired." Says Kera.

"I'll be back, sis. Time is ticking. I got stuff to do." She says.

"Okay, okay. Go then, and stop talking to me." Says Kera.

"Oh, shut up! I'm going." Says Julissa,

Well Julissa is in the shower. Kera's man texts her, and says he has bad news, andhe's going to have to cancel the plans this time. She quickly responds back with a, Huh? Are you serious? He sends a message back! Yes, boo, I have to go to Japan today to sign this client. He is ready to sign these papers. That is my job sexy, I have to go to Japan today! Unless, you want to gowith me? I would love the company.

Wait, what? Japan? That is crazy! She texts back saying, I missed the flight already.Well, the jet leaves at 9:00 A.M. if you change your mind. Atlanta airport follows the signs that say private, and it will send you directly to the jet. His text says.

Damn, I don't know. I'm going to think about it. I will text you in a few minutes.Kera text back

Okay, let me know. He texts back.

"Julissa! OMG you would not guess what just happened!" Kera yells as she walks to thebathroom.

Julissa getting out of the shower says, "What? What?"

"Well, Julian just texted me, and said he's not going to be able to spend the day withme because he has to fly to Japan today to meet with the client to sign some very important papers." Says Kera.

"Oh, say less, so he can't chill with you?"

"Girl, that is not it. He said I can go with him. He invited me to get on his private jetto go with him for the day to Japan. We will be back tonight." Says Kera.

"What? You're actually thinking of going?" Julissa asks a she raises one of her eyebrows.

"Oh, no sis. You don't know him well enough to go out the country with him even if it's for a day." Julissa says.

"Julissa, I really wanted to spend the day with him. He says he's going for work," says Kera.

"Yes, love, maybeso, but you can't trust him." Says Julissa.

"I hear you, but I've never been to Japan it might be fun." Says Kera.

"Yeah, and it could cost you everything. Honestly, I would not go, but you are a grown ass woman. And you not going to listen anyway." Says Julissa, "I know you too well."

"I don't think he will ask me to go to work in a private jet. I'll be okay, sis. I really want to go. I will stay in touch with you the entire time."

"You better." Says Julissa, "themoment I can't reach you I'm calling the cops!"

"Okay Liz, I understand. I will keep you informed at all times." Kera nods.

"Like I said, you better. I don't want to lose you, girl. I love you."

"Love you too, girl."

"All right, I got to get dressed to go to work." Julissa says as she goes into the bedroom, and grab some clothes. She picked out a pair of blue slacks, and a blouseto match. Grabs her bag, and heads to the kitchen to grab a cup of coffee on the way out. She poured it into her to-go tumbler, because it will stay warm on herway to work. She goes toward the full door, and quickly turns around, and goes to hug Kera. She tells her to stay in touch, and she wants to know when she gets to the airport. Her flight boards, and then when she lands.

"What part of Japan arey'all going to?" She asked.

"All I know is he said Japan." Says Kera.

"Well that is something else. I need to know before you go. Send me the info soon." Says Julissa, "Okay, love I got to go, but call when you get that info no matter what, or text it if I don't answer." She waves back as she walks out the door, and into the elevator. Just that shewalks out, and to the elevator, her phone rings.

It is her mama. "Hey, boo bear, Kera's leaving today, right?" She asked.

"No, mom. She's staying until tomorrow."

"Oh, okay. Maybe, I'll see her today!" She says.

"Probably not, because she's spending the day with her new guy friend, Julio." Says Julissa.

"Oh, okay, well… I guess I won't then!"Mama Lucky says while Julissa gets on the elevator just in time. Once inside, Dennis and big Joe are inside going down too.

"Hey, sexy." Says Dennis.

"Good morning, Miss Julissa, excuse him. He hasn't had his coffee yet." Says big Joe.

"Oh, no worries, I know he's harmless."

"Are you heading into the office?" Big Joe asks.

"Yes, I am. I have a meeting at 10:00." Says Julissa.

"Oh, okay."

"What about you Mr. Michaels?"

"Just a regular day for me," says Dennis.

Elevator stops at the first floor and Big Joe leaves to go retrieve the vehicle, and then follows

Julissa. "Hey, girl, wait up! Why are you walking all fast?"

"What, Dennis?"

"Are you still with that zero? When are you going to come back to me, I'll be your hero." Says Dennis.

"That was solame. *You* are the zero Dennis. Stop bothering me! I don't have time for you and your shenanigans today. I have to go!"

"Bye, then, Miss Lucky." as Big Joe drives up hegets in as Julissa walks away.

"Boss you need to leave that woman alone. She's not the one to play with. The dude she's with is pretty big in Georgia."

"Whatever, I'm not doing anything. Just speaking to the woman." Says Dennis.

"Yeah, boss, but she's your boss now. You have to show her some respect."

"Oh, shut up, I'm your boss, you have to listen to me, too." Says Dennis.

"Sure thing, boss." Says Big Joe, "I will shut the hellup!"

"Good thing, now take me to work before I'm late and get fired. Which can't happen. They need me!"

Julissa drives in to work and gets there right before Dennis. As she walks in, she is greeted as usual by the employees. She walks into her office and takes a quick glimpse to see Mr. Prince was in his office.

"Meeting in ten minutes!" he yells across the hall to Julissa.

"Yes, sir, I will be ready, boss."

"Thank you."

"No problem, BP. Got to keep you on your toes," he adds.

"Of course you do. Miss Jennifer, can you come to my office?" She says.

"Yes, ma'am," as she comes to the door.

"Can you please go into the conference room, and prepare coffee, and lay out the workbooks for us says?" Julissa says.

"No problem, Miss Lucky, right away." Says Jennifer as she goes toward the conference room.

"Hey, Jen. How are you today?" Says Jerome from Accounting Department.

"I'm great. It's a beautiful day! Got to go. Talk to youlater," says Jennifer.

"Okay, no problem, later then." He replies.

Julissa waits a few more minutes, and then goes on to the conference room. Hoping she makes it there before anyone else. And it just so happens she did, then everyone else shows up. The main part of the meeting was to talk about the new campaign.

It was a newborn campaign, coming to Atlanta, called 'Molasses' and they will be using Dennis as the spokesperson for the new newsletter. Plus, he will also be traveling a lot. Because they have several buildings around the world. Miss Lucky, I need you to go and get Mr. Michaels. He needs to hear this!"

"Yes, sure thing, right away." Says Julissa as she quickly gets up to go and find Dennis. She walks around a bit, because he wasn't at his desk then he comes back.

He says, "Are you looking for me, Miss Lucky? I knew I was wearing you down."

"Whatever, Dennis, this is all about business. We need you in the conference room." She says.

"I will be right there." He says.

"Okay, see you in there." She says and then walks back to the conference room, and a few seconds later Mr. Michaels also walks in.

"Mr. Michaels, we wanted you to join us because as you already know, we are accepting a new campaign. It is called 'Molasses'. It's a new club coming to ATL. And they would like you to be the spokesperson for the club. You will represent them, and all of the States that they promote. You will be doing a lot of traveling now. So, make sure you have everything ready. You will have a monthly calendar and 'Molasses' will cover all of your expenses; housing, car, flights, everything. Here is Mr. Gerald Evans, he will fill you in with all the details. He is the CEO of 'Molasses'. You two can talk as you walk to the side. Well I told you all it would be a quick meeting. You are all free to go if I have any extra info. I will send it in an email."

Everyone agrees, and they all leave. Mr. Prince and Julissa go back to their offices, and then Julissa decides to check her emails before leaving while scrolling through she has a new email from Mr. Prince, with the subject 'Important message'. She opens it and it says, you will need to help Mr. Michaels.

Julissa goes and knocks on his door to see why. Mr. Prince invites her in and says, "I see you got the email!"

'Yes, what do I need to help him with?"

"Isn't Mr. Evans helping him with everything?" She asked.

"Yes, but since you know him so well, I need you to keep an eye on him on these trips, and make sure he decides to come back. These people wanted to sign him badly, so I hope they are not trying to take him from us on the slide."

"Wait, what? I'm going to be traveling with this man?" says Miss Lucky.

"Yes," says Mr. Prince, "Exactly, Miss Lucky. A great idea. I was thinking maybe just talk to him, but your idea sounds more promising. We need him to stay around. He has brought in a lot of extra money here." Says Mr. Prince.

"Oh, wow, Mr. Prince that is asking a lot. Why can't we give one of the other staff a promotion, and have them stay with him. Don't you need me to be here?" Asks Julissa.

"Well, if you can find me someone I will send them. I do need you here. But I'll handle, if you need to go."

"All right, then, I'll get on it right away!" She says.

"We'll make it quick because his flight to Birmingham, Alabama, is in 3 days. He will be traveling before the building here is finished." He says.

"Okay, I'll keep that in mind." She says.

"You do that." He says, "Aren't you leaving?"

"Yes, actually, I don't need to stay. Do you need me for anything?"

"No, I already had your day off covered. Now, go and enjoy your day. Bye!"

"Well, bye, then. Guess, I'll go get some lunch." As she was leaving the building, she got a few text messages from Kera. She must have sent them while she was in the office, she thought.

One message said, we will be in Tokyo, Japan. And another one said, our flight leaves at 10:00 A.M. The last one said, we areboarding the plane now. Love you, Liz. I will see you when I get back. Don't worry, I will text, and keep my location on.

Julissa looks at the time, and sees that it's 11:20 A.M. She quickly starts to panic. "Oh my God. I can't believe she went! She doesn't know this guy." She then texts back, what is his name? I know Jaleel, but Jaleel, what? She then drives back to her suite.

As she is getting off the elevator. She sees Tim.

"Hi, babe. What are you doing here? I thought you would be at the airport." Tim says.

"No, Kera is staying another day."

"Oh, okay, y'all going to lunch?"

"No, she kind of went to Tokyo."

"She went where? Japan? For what? Work?" He asked.

"Nope, following her new dude." She says.

"She doing it like that? Damn I hope she's okay."

"Yes, me too. You know what I want to get my mind off of her for now. Are you busy?" She asked.

"No, what do you want to do?" He asked.

"Let's go to yoursuite. You have anything to eat?" She asked.

"No, I was just about to get something." He says, "Let's order something and get it delivered."

"Okay. Let's do that." As they walked to his suite. He opens the door, and Julissa goes in and sits on the couch.

Tim asks her, "Would you like a drink or a snack? I'm getting a snack."

"Yes, I'll take a drink. Wine, perhaps, what are we doing ordering to eat?" She asks.

"I don't know. I was figuring seafood."

She says, "I like that idea. You go ahead and order some crab legs, and of course, some shrimp with corn and potatoes. My fave, but you should know that." Shesays.

"Yes, I already ordered online. It will be here in 30 minutes." He says, then comesback with a bag of potato chips, her wine, and a glass of tea, then sits down beside Julissa. He then turns on the TV to find a movie or something to watch. Looks over atJulissa only to find that she is giving him the 'I want you look!'

Not soon after, she jumps on his lap, pushes him back on the couch, and starts to kiss him. At first, he is kind of hesitant, but then she quickly convinces him, and he kisses her back. He then grabs her, picks her up, and puts her on the counter. Then he starts ripping off her clothes, and then soon Julissa's buck naked, lying flat on the counter. Tim goes to the fridge and brings out some whipped cream, and grapes. He feeds her a grape, and sprays the cream on her breasts and vagina. She wiggles a little because it was so cool, but it felt so good then she starts moaning softly. Tim then grabs a hold of her breasts, and slowly grips and puts his face in her Fiona, and starts to lick whipped cream and her vagina. She keeps wiggling because with every leg it tickles oh so good! He keeps licking so long that delicious insides feel almost raw, and then all of a sudden she starts to squirt and screams.

"I am about to come. Oh my gosh! It is coming now, baby. Don't stop. Please don't stop!" Her grip on his face gets tighter as she lets out the sexiest moan he had ever heard from her, and then he instantly feels a gush of fluids come down into his face, and tongue. He just kept licking and Julissa was moaning so hard the people in the next suite started banging on the wall, and he just kept licking till she comes again, and literally slides off the counter.

She then gets up and pushes him down on the couch, and kisses his lips with a sloppy kiss, and then moving down to his manhood, and begins to lick all around the tip, and slowly slides her mouth over the top and slides all the way down. Tim is feeling some type of way from how good her mouth feels. He grabs her head as she comes up, and pushes her back down. She then begins to suck it hard, as she goes up and down. Trying to make the sneakers green, but he moans a lot.

She keeps it up until he grabs your hair, and then she knows what's about to happen, so she pulls back up a bit, and then as soon as she feels becoming she grips it tight, and let it come. Tim is literally sensitive as hell as she continues to grip his dick and takes all of it. Has she moved what way he is tensing up because it gets extra sensitive now.

She then puts Julissa on top of his lap and she starts kissing him hoping it won't take forever to get him back up. She really wants him to get inside her. She wants to ride. The kissing is not working fast enough. So she starts to think, and plays with this dick, and after a few minutes he is back up.

She then raises up on top of his dick and slides down! She starts to go faster, and as she is just about to come, he picks her up, and lays her down on the couch. Just as he lays her on the couch there is a knock at the door.

"It must be the food," says Tim. "Wait one minute, babe." As he goes to the door, Julissa plays with her ass, naked on the couch. He opens the door, and the guy at the door can literally see Julissa on the couch and Tim is behind the door also naked. He tells a guy to leave it at the door and quickly shuts it, and waits a few minutes then looks out to see if anyone is out there.

There is no one, so he grabs the bags and takes them inside, puts them on the counter, and goes right back to Julissa. Grab her legs, pull her down towards him, slowly slides inside her, and slowly starts to stroke in and out of her. She grabs his face and kisses his lips.

At this point, he is still stroking slower than he takes the right leg and slides it over his shoulders and starts going faster, as he does this, Julissa is pushing back, and making the strokes tighter as she squeezes her vagina over his dick. All of a sudden Julissa starts to flow down her foot. It feels funny, but she just keeps going. It wasn't very long after that Tim starts to tense up, and before she has time to speak up, Julissa grabs his shoulders, tightens her thighs, and says she's coming.

The sensation was so strong that they both moaned and satisfaction and then Tim lays down beside her, and they both try to catch their breath. They laid there for a little bit before Tim jumps up, and goes to the restroom, and uses it, washes his hands, and go straight to the kitchen and to the food.

He looks over at Julissa and finds her fast asleep. He calls out, "Babe, I know you're hungry. Get up and come get this while it's hot."

Julissa open her eyes from her little cat nap and go to the kitchen, wash her hands, and easily starts eating. She grabbed a crab leg, and broke it and sucked out all the meat with the juices.

Tim was like, "Damn! Let me take it to the table. Looks like you're going to need some room. Girl, you tore up that crab leg."

They both sit down at the table and devour that food. After they are done, both wash their hands, grab the rest of their drinks, and move to the couch after they clean up.

"Well, babe, I hate to eat and run, but I need to go to my suite. I need a shower and check on Kera. She's been with that nigga alone for too long already."

She then gets up, grabs her bag, leans over, and kisses Tim on the cheek, then leaves. She goes on back to her suite and calls Kera.

First call goes to voicemail. Second call she picks up. "Girl, are you okay?" She says.

'Yes, Liz. I am having the best time here. Tokyo is so beautiful. We are actually thinking of coming back tomorrow night instead of the morning. So we can take in the sites and food here." Kera says.

"What? Oh, no. Don't you have to get back to work? You said one more day! Not two."

"Yes, I know but I've already told them I'll be there on Monday morning. I'm off on the weekends, anyway." Says Kera.

"Shit, Monday? You're still coming back tomorrow though. Maybe we can spend a few more days together before Monday."

"Of course, I will be back tomorrow, but not morning. We are taking the afternoon flight and won't be back and won't make it back to ATL till that night." Says Kera.

"Okay, okay. You already got me nervous over here, but Tim kind of was able to take my mind off of things for a minute. Girl he just gave me an afternoon delight. We were all over the bed, the kitchen counters, the sofa."

"So, like, how y'all used to be." She says.

"Oh, well, yes, but, girl, this was way better."

"Anyways, Liz, I got to go! We will talk more when I get back. Jaleel and I are about to have a late lunch, and go and see around a little before dark. Maybe some shopping too. Girl, this man has got his shit together. This might get kind of serious."

"Just be careful, boo. Love you. Have fun, and please stay alert. If not of him, his people, and surroundings."

"Okay, Liz, I will. Bye for now." Julissa gets off the line, and goes and takes off her clothes and gets into the shower. Water is just steaming up the windows. She gets in and just lets the water fall on her face and down her body. She stays there for like 30 to 45 minutes. By the time she decides to get out, it is almost 2:00 P.M. She looks at the clock on the wall. She decides to take a nap. Tim really worked her out. She thought as she grabbed her towel, and dries off then grabs a negligee out of the drawer, and slides it on, and lays on the bed. She kept thinkingwhat got into him. She just kept yawning, and then instantly fell to sleep.

Julissa is sleeping so well. She slept a long time because she was exhausted. Her phone rings, and it is her sister. She is a bit tired so she lets it ring. Then it rang again. This time she answers it.

"Hey, sis, what are you doing tonight?" She asked.

"Oh, nothing right now. I saw Tim earlier. So, I probably won't see him tonight. What didyou have in mind?" Julissa replied.

"Oh there is a work party I have to attend tonight and the hubby can't go because he has to go to work. So I was seeing if my little sis would like to join me instead."

"Work party? I don't know. Will there be food?"

"Yes, of course, sis. If not, I wouldn't be going 'cuz I got to eat. It's not really a work thing but all people I work with will be there, so that's why I say work party." She says.

"Sure, what are youwearing?" Julissa asks.

"Oh, probably some jeans, and a cute V-neck shirt and some heels,cute ones." she says.

"Oh, okay. I'll do the same, or maybe I'll put on one of the new outfits I bought on my little work vacay." She says.

"All right, sis, be ready at six, I will be there to pick you up."

"Okay, see you then, as they both hang up. Julissa then goes to her closet, and looks for one of the outfits she just bought. It was a cute little two-piece set. All black, everything. She found a cute little jewelry set to go with it. She goes and grabs a glass of wine, and sits down on the couch. It was early, so she had time to relax for a while.

As she is surfing for something, she gets acall from her brother, Alex. "Hey, Alex. What do you want?" She asked.

"Oh, nothing, sis. I was just calling to invite you to a barbecue at my place."

"Okay. When?" She said.

"Sunday. Tanae has to work on Saturday."

"All right, I'll be there, what time?"

"2:00 P.M. cuz I know we all got to be at work on Monday." He says.

"Okay, cool. I'll be there. Is Mom going?"

"I don't know. I haven't called her yet. I wanted to call you first." He says.

"I guess, you better call her! She will never cook for you again, if you don't." She says.

"I know right, sis. I'm going to call her as soon as we get off the phone. Good night, sis. See you Sunday."

"Sure thing, good night, bro." Julissa says as she hangs up, she then decides to watch a movie. She still had about 3 hours till Sissy would be there to pick her up. Finally she stopped flipping.

She found an old movie, *Stomp the Yard,* she started watching the movie, and received a text so she picked up her phone, and texted back. It was from Tim.

Babe, are you okay? You left so suddenly. I had to check on you.

Yes, I am fine. Watching a movie. Going to some dinner party with my sister at 6:00. What are you up to?

He then calls. "Hey, babe. So, a dinner party?"

"Yes, with her work friends she asked me to go with her because her husband won't be able to go. He has to work as usual. I guess he's on night shifts again, so there will be most likely a lot of me tagging along. Oh, yeah! Alex is having a barbecue on Sunday. You want to go?" She asked.

"I'll let you know, because I was supposed to go to my mom's. I was going to invite you."

"That's funny but I will understand if you can't or maybe we can make both. Just a suggestion." She says.

"Well, she might cancel. It was discussed. Not confirm yet." He says, "Okay, babe. I will."

"I'm going to watch the rest of the movie." She says.

"What movie and would you like some company?"

"*Stomp the Yard…* and no, if you come over, we won't be watching the movie. My coochie still needs a break." With a smile on her face.

"My bad then. Enjoy the movie!" He says rudely.

"Nothing personal, but babe, you had me tired." She explains that is just what you do to me."

"But remember, you started it," he says.

"Okay, okay, talk to you soon. I'm hanging up now. I'll call you after."

"Sure you will," he says, "X's and O's X's and O's. Bye." Then he hangs up.

Julissa continues to watch the movie and gets all comfortable on the couch and falls asleep. She keeps waking up on certain parts of the movie, but then wakes on up and gets another glass of wine. She then keeps watching the rest of the movie and then looks at the time. It is almost 5:00 p.m. and she needs to start getting dressed. She walks into her bathroom and turns on the two-in-one curling and straightening iron, and then sits down on the toilet. She finishes up then washes her hands and dries them and starts on her hair. She adds a few curls as usual with the lot of bounce.

She then goes into the bedroom to put on her clothes. Looking at the time, it is now 5:45. Knowing her sister will be here soon, she then picks up a pair of shoes, and puts them on. Snaps her necklace clasp and slides on two gold bracelet bracelets. She goes to her mirror and checks herself out. She puts a stamp of approval, and goes to the front room to wait for her sister. About 20 minutes later, she knocks on the door. Julissa answers and then walks out with her sister.

They get downstairs. She was parked in the front. They drive on to the restaurant. The party is a surprise birthday party Julissa and her sister had a great time. Julissa fit right in with the work folks. Time went by so fast that before they knew it, it was time to go. Julissa and her sister both said goodbye to everyone, and walked out to the car and got in. It was a bit cold now.

The weather totally had changed. They drove, went to Julissa's and she hugged her sister and got out and went inside and up to her suite. Once inside she grabs a glass of wine, because she was not sleepy yet. Set down on her bed and checked her phone to see if Kera sent anyone messages. She had sent her a 'good night, boo' about 9:45 P.M. Happy to see a message from her She then sent one back saying, 'good night. Love you. Can't wait to see you tomorrow night. And be careful.' She finishes up her wine, and turn on the news to see what crazy shit happened in ATLtoday, and then made herself go to sleep by turning off the light, and closing her eyes.

Chapter 14

The Surprise Dinner

It is about 3:00 A.M., and Julissa is sound asleep. So sound that she didn't even hearher phone ring about three times. As the last ring comes through, she kind of couldhear something, and so she wakes up.

Sounding like crap, she answers the phone. "Hello?"

The line was so scratchy, she couldn't even hear the person on the other line, but even she figured that it was Kera.

"Liz, why are you sleeping?" Kara says.

"Oh, maybe because it is like three in thedamn morning. Girl, what do you want? I am tired! Why are you calling me this early in the morning?"

The phone goes all scratchy again as she is explaining, and Julissa, not really hearing her say, "All right. Okay, no problem."

"Well, I love you, see you later." Kera says, "See you when I get home.Bye," as she hangs up.

Julissa rolls back over, and goes back to sleep. Her 6:00 A.M. alarm goes off, and knowing she has to get up for work, she jumps on up. She hears a knock at the door. She goes to the door, and checks the peep hole to see who it is. Once she checks, she sees that it is her new neighbor, Miss Angie from next door. Really sweetlady, she thought. The other lady that was there moved out about a week ago. The lady kept knocking, and Julissa then opened the door.

"Hey, Miss, I really need a favor."

"Okay," says Julissa, "how can I help you?"

"I need a ride to work. You think you can help me out? My car is in the shop until tomorrow. It was supposed to be out today, but they found an oil leak that needs tobe fixed, but not until later today, maybe tomorrow!" She says.

"I have to be in by 9:00 A.M." says Angie.

"Well, I need to be at work by 8:00 A.M. I can drop you off on the way. If you don'tmind being an hour early?"

"Oh no, that will be fine! I can be ready by 7:15."

"Okay, Miss Angie, I'll see you at 7:20. That should give you a little extra time."

"Okay, thank you. I'll be ready," as she walks back to her suite a few doors down.

Julissa closes the door and walks to her kitchen to start a coffee pot until she realizes she needs to buy coffee. Thinking… Oh, I'll get some today on my way home after work. She grabs a bottle of water, and takes a couple sips, and walks into the living room and turns on the TV. She just has to see what happened in ATL last night. As usual she flips, and flips till she sees her favorite news channel. Mr. Nightit's her every time.

112

She thinks as she watches his skills. Damn that man knows he is fine! She thought he had the best smile, and that beautiful black skin! Oh my, she sits through a few more stories, but nothing too interesting, so she turns off the TV, and grabs her water then goes to the bedroom. She sits on her bed, and starts her normal daydreaming, but she quickly snaps out of it!

She gets up, and goes to the shower and turns on the water. She lets it run for a little while, and she gets on in the water. It feels so good. She forgot her towel, so she quietly gets out and steps onto the floor with her wet feet, leaving wet footprints all the way to and from the closet. She walks back to the shower making even more wet footprints on the floor.I'll dry that when I'm done, she thought.

Once she gets back in the water it feels so good. She takes her washcloth and once it is wet enough she starts to wash her body. First, she washes the higher parts, and then she goes down to the lower parts. While in the shower, there is another knock at the door. Really needing to finish, she continues towash. Again a few more times there goes that knock again.

Completely irritated, she again gets out of the shower, wet feet, and all. Grab her towel and goes to thedoor, and rudely asks, "Who is it? I was in the shower?"

The voice from behind the doorsounded like Dennis. She then opens the door and says, "What do you want, Dennis?I need to finish my shower," as she cracks the door open just a little.

"Oh, my, so you are naked behind this door? Why don't you invite me in, with your sexy ass body and hair dripping wet. You know what I would be doing, if I was in there, right now. As you came to the door, and saw who was out there. I would be slipping my fingers under that towel, and making you moan at this door. Not caringwho was there. I would be pushing my fingers in and out and playing with that clit that you would have to close the door. Once you close the door, I would take off that towel. Lay it on the floor, and then I would be eating up that pussy, girl. I would devour it."

Julissa standing here, horny as hell at that moment, says, "Damn, Dennis. Stop!"

"Why do you want me to stop? Are you afraid you might want to fulfill my fantasy?"He asks.

"No, I wouldn't. Anyways, what do you want? I am pretty sure I already asked youthat question, but really now, what is it?" She asks.

"Can I get a ride with you to work? Big Joe had an emergency and had to go to South Carolina yesterday. I was meaning to ask Jerome yesterday, but it slipped mymind. I could just take an Uber but I thought I would at least try to ask. Ok, so whatdo you say? Please? Do you mind?"

"Yes, I do mind, but only because Big Joe had an emergency. I will take you. I amleaving at 7:20. I also have someone else riding with me so you will have to get inthe back."

"Okay, no problem. Thank you. I will be ready," as he goes back to his suite.Just as he walks in Tim shows up from around the corner.

"Hey, babe." She says.

"Good morning, beautiful." He says "I was just coming to see you. I wasn't able tosee you last night so I brought you some breakfast."

"Oh, babe. That was so sweet, but I have been having so many interruptions that Ineed to finish my shower first."

"Okay, babe. Go ahead." He slaps her on her butt on the way past him.

"Oh!" She says, "That stung a little!"

"Babe, go and finish! I'll still be here." He grabs the remote, and turns on the TV. Julissa goes back to her shower. She finishes up, and quickly gets out. By now itis getting late, and she still needs to blow dry her hair, she thought.

"Babe, I heard thewater turn off. You need me to dry you off?" Ask Tim.

"No, babe, if you come in here Iwill never get dressed. I have to get out of here about 7:15 today. I have to take myneighbor to work this morning. Her car is in the shop." She says.

"Oh, so do you want me to pack your breakfast to go?"

"What time is it?" She asked.

He looks at his watch, and says, "It's 6:45."

"Oh shit!" She says, "I am going to have to speed up the process quite a bit, I had to blow dry my hair and get dressed still."

"Okay, babe. I'm going to fix it all to go." Says Tim.

"Thankfully," she says, "I will be out in a few minutes."

"You sure you don't need anyhelp there?" Ask Tim.

"I'm sure," says Julissa.

"Okay, just thought you could use some help!" Says Tim.

"Time?" Asked Julissa.

"7:00," he says.

"Okay, I just need to throw on my clothes." She had already picked out some blackpants, and a white and black blouse, with some black shoes.

Julissa grabs a belt, and a necklace as she walks toward the living room. Grabs thefood that Tim has packaged. Gives him a kiss, and a huge hug and go outside, and as she gets ready to get on the elevator, Miss Angie comes out of her suite and they both get on the elevator together.

"Thank you for being ready."

"Oh, no problem. You are doing me a favor. I wasjust watching TV, and looking at the clock. You came out earlier than 7:20, but it'sokay cuz as I said I was already ready." Says Miss Angie.

They get to the first floor, and walk out to Julissa's car.

Julissa sits and waits for Dennis because she knows he's coming as well.

'We have to wait for one more," Julissa says.

"Oh, no problem," says Miss Angie. Just then, Dennis walks up to the car and jumps inthe backseat and closes the door and they drive off. A few minutes later, they make it to Miss Andy's job. Julissa is about to drop heroff.

She says, "Thank you and goodbye." But Julissa stops her.

"Would you be needing a ridehome?" Julissa so sweetly asked.

"Oh no, I'll just get a ride home with the coworker." Angie says.

"Are you sure? I don't mind if you need me." Says Julissa.

"Yes, I'm sure, plus my car should be ready by today, so I might just be getting a ridestraight there anyways. I mean it better be done! I need my car!" Angie says.

Julissa says, "Okay, and well here is my number just in case you need me," she says as she grabs a piece of paper from her notepad, and writes her number and hands it to her.She then gets out, and says bye. Julissa then drives off to her job.

Can I get in the front?" Asks Dennis.

"No, stay back there You're good."

Fortunately there was not much traffic so they made it there in no time. They wereso early that Mr. Prince was opening up the building. She decided to sit a little longer before going in, but Dennis decided to go inside.

Looking at the time. It is 7:50. Mr. Prince is late she thought

After a few more minutes, she figured he was sitting in his office. So he gets out ofher car, and goes inside.

Mr. Prince comes out of the conference room and says, "Hey, Miss Lucky. How areyou doing this morning? This beautiful day?"

"Oh, I am doing really well. I just really miss my friend. Oh, okay let's keep yourmind off of that. Go and do the morning announcements."

"No problem, Mr. Prince, but what do we need to announce today? Anything new?"

He hands her a note card, and says, "it's all there," and walks away.

"Oh, so you already had this planned?" She says.

"No, and yes," he says as he turns the corner to go into his office.

She then looks at the no card. The list read: Mr. Michaels - campaign / Paris onTuesday.

New weeks issue - *One Take* sections.

A new, weekly person of the week rather than month helps more people to try for it.Everything else still applies.

She then re-reads the first note. Paris, with Dennis? She thought Omg! I need to talk to Mr. Prince, and or find someone quick that can take that trip instead of me.She thought.

Everyone starts arriving. It is almost 8:15 A.M., and Julissa announces time for morning announcements!

Everyone then goes to the conference room, waits on Julissa to start. She startstalking about Mr. Michaels, and his Paris trip. "I thought I would have more notice, but okay, I have never been there."

Dennis says, "Might be fun."

"Okay, next thing, we are changing the employee of the month to employ of the week." Says Julissa.

Everyone claps, and says, "Yeah! Now it will give us more chances to get it!"

"Yes, exactly." Julissa said, "So that also means, you all need to work harder, and show us what y'all can do! It also means more jobs and more promotions if it works out." She talked about a few more topics from the note card, and dismissed everyone. She walks toward her office, and Mr. Prince calls her into his office.

"I'm sure you know you will be accompanying Mr. Michaels?"

"Yes, but you said, if I find someone else to go then they can go in my place right?"

"Yes, but it's only for a few days. Get over there. Help. And watch him, then get back. I'm sure you can do that? Am I right? Or do I need to search for a new VP?"

"Yes, I can go, but I really would prefer not to. Plus, don't you remember him saying he doesn't want to do business without you?"

"Oh, I've already spoken with Mr. Michaels. He is totally on board. Well, it took a little convincing, but we came to an understanding." He says.

"Oh, okay, but I have a few days to find someone so I will try at least." Says Julissa.

"You do what you can, but I'm sure you just need to prepare to leave for at least three days." He says.

"Okay, Mr. Prince. I give up! We both know there is no one else here to send on a trip like that." She says, "Plus, it would be nice to see Paris."

"Okay, Miss Lucky. Now we have an understanding. Go, and get to work. Planning out your next few days of work. I will be giving you Monday off so that you can be prepared for your trip!"

How the hell am I going to break this to Tim, she thought. I can tell him about the work trip, but I definitely cannot tell him who I am going with. Then she kept overthinking, oh my god, how on earth, am I going to be in the same gorgeous country with Dennis? I will keep my distance, she thought some more.

Jerome comes, knocks on her door, and she snaps out of it!

"Miss Lucky, I was just wondering what we are having for lunch today? I haven't seen the new calendar yet."

"Oh, okay, how about we do subs? I'm about to call, and get them delivered by 11:45."

"Thank you, and if you have the new calendar, I would be happy to take it, and put it up for you."

"Yes, I have it right here," she gives the new calendar to him, and he walks out of her office and goes down the hall to the break room desk drawer and gets a thumbtack and pushes it into the calendar and puts it on the wall.

Julissa she looked up the number on the subway to order some subs for the office. She ordered more than thirty subs. Set to be delivered by lunch time, which was 11:45 for the office. It is now 10:00 and everyone is working hard, because they are just trying to get this issue of the magazine out by today. So that possibly they can be off tomorrow. Julissa is hard at work and her office Mr. Prince is in a very important call. Even Jennifer is busy. I guess Mr. Prince telling them that they will be off tomorrow put some fire under them. She hadn't heard from her all day knowing she was supposed to be flying in tonight, she thought.

Julissa picks up her phone to call Kera but she didn't answer the first time, Julissa calls her back. She still didn't answer, but instead, she textsback saying, I'm watching a movie with Jaleel. Can I call you later? Love you.

Wait, a movie? Isn't it like almost time for you your flight home? She texts.

No, Liz. I told you this morning. We were going to stay another night, she texts back.

No, no, no you didn't tell me that! Well I was kind of out of it so you might have,but why? You need to be home, I mean here, she texts.

Well, let's say that we are really enjoying Miami. Loving life over here. I'm actually thinking about moving, anyways, we can talk about it tomorrow. We will be back inATL around 5:00 P.M. she texts.

Oh, I guess. Girl, I hope you are being careful. You still don't really know thisman.

Julissa put her phone away and looks at the clock seeing that it is time for lunch. The food should be here bynow. She thought.

She then texts back, I will text you in a little while. About to have some lunch.

Okay Liz, love you, see you tomorrow! She texts.

Just as she lays down her phone, and walks to her lobby, there is a ringing of the doorbell. It was a subway employee delivering the food. She buzzes them through, and they bring all of the sandwiches inside. It took about three trips to bring all the food. There were a lot of sandwiches. Well, they dropped them off, and it is alreadylunch time so everyone stops at a stopping point, and goes and gets a sandwich, chips, and a drink each.

Julissa and Mr. Prince then go and get theirs, and both go back to their offices. Everyone sits down to eat, and then they soon are done, and ready to get back towork.

Time seems to fly by, and it is now 3:45 P.M. Time for Julissa to prepare to leave for the day. She starts her process and her day. Turns off the computer. Does her rounds to find out that a few people are still not even close to being done. Kind of upset she doesn't really want to come in tomorrow. But she has to report back to Mr.Prince.

She then reports to everyone that they will need to be at work tomorrow, but theyare free to go for the day, and they will be compensated for their last hour. Absolutely no one hesitates to get out of there, the employees are happy, and it wasn't long before everyone was gone.

It was now a few minutes till 4:00, and Julissa finished up. And leaves thebuilding.

She gets in her car and gets a call. "Hey, baby," she says, "what's up? You time that justright! I just sat down in my car."

"Oh, nothing, but my mom would like to have us over for dinner tonight and then Ifigured we could go home and relax. I know you have had a long day! Well I figured that."

"Actually baby I need to talk to you, so we can do that once I get home, get therebefore we go to your mom's." She says.

"All right, babe. Is everything okay?" He asked.

"Nothing bad. Just something we need to talk about."

"Okay, I'll see you once you gethere."

"Just come to my suite," he says.

"No you come to mine. I'll see you soon, babe. Bye." She says asshe hangs up.

Julissa drives to her suite, and all the while hoping he is not upset. She finallygets to the hotel. She drives up to the parking, and once done, gets out of her car and goes inside. Tim is already downstairs to meet her. He grabs her by the hand, and they walk towards the elevator and get on, as Tim presses the floor button someone comes into the elevator. It is Miss Angie.

She says, "Thank you, Julissa, for taking me to work this morning. I really appreciate it. I had a friend take me to pick up my car. It's right outside. If you ever need anything, don't hesitate to ask."

They make it up to their floor, and they all get off and go separate ways.

Tim and Julissa goes to her suite. She quietly sits down, and says, "Babe, I need togo to Paris for three days on Tuesday for my job! One of our clients has to go for a campaign, and I have to go to keep an eye on them." She explains.

"Oh, no way! Babe… Paris without me? Well, I will miss you, but if it's for work itmust be important," he says.

Julissa says, "For real, baby? You're not mad?"

"Mad? How can I be mad? That would be so stupid. I mean you have to work just like I do. No, baby, you go ahead, and do your job! Just be careful. Hopefully, you allhave a bodyguard with you at all times. Better have one!" He says.

She goes and kisses him and says, "Thank you for understanding, babe. Mr. Princesays only three days, but I don't have to go till Tuesday. I will be back on Friday. Tuesday we get there, Wednesday is our official first day for the campaign."

"Oh, okay, babe. I need you to shower and put something nice on." He says hechanges the subject.

Julissa goes to her closet, and picks out a cute dress. She was trying to match him. He was looking extra fine in a black button-down, and slacks. She picked outa black dress and some heels.

She then gets into the shower. As she starts washing up, outside, Tim grabs a black tiny box out of his pocket, and just has to look at it one more time.

The big ass grin on his face says it all!

Julissa quickly gets out of the shower and grabsfor her towel. Tim sees her trying to grab it, and he starts pushing it farther back so she can'treach it. He pushes it so far that she has to get out completely naked.

Looking at his lady's body. He starts oohing and eyeing, but she gets her towel, andcovers up knowing they have no time to play.

"Oh, I'll get you later." He says. Julissa dries off and gets dressed.Tim goes back to the living room.

Julissa grabs her bag, and shoes and goes in there with him. She gives him hershoes. She needs him to put them on for her, because of the straps. He puts them on as he tries to slide his hands under her dress.

She playfully yells, "Stop! We need to go!"

"Yes, but oh, never mind. Let's go."

They leave the hotel, and drive to Tim's mom's house. There are so many cars onthe street. Guessing the other houses must have a party going on or something they get outand going inside.

As they get inside. Julissa says hi to his mom, and she gives her really soft sweethug and she says hello back.

Tim then excuses himself to go to the bathroom, but instead he goes to the bedroom. Julissa's mom and everyone else is in the bedroom. He tells everyone tobe quiet, and he will be back.

He then leaves the room and walks back out and turns on some music, and grabs Julissa by the hand. He lets her know how much he loves her and he would do anything for her.

Tim's mom goes and tells everyone to come out, and as they do Julissa nearly drops her lip, "What are y'all doing here? I thought that car lookedfamiliar, Alex? Hi, Tanae, girls. OMG, Tim?"

"Baby, as I was saying before being interrupted. Would you make me the happiestman alive and say you will be my wife?" He then take out a small black box from his pocket, and then from it, a gorgeous diamond ring!

"Oh my gosh, Tim. We have to talk!"

"Baby, just say yes, boo bear." Says mama Lucky.

"Yes, Tim, yes, baby! I will marry you!" She exclaims loudly in happiness as he puts a ring on her finger. "It's beautiful,Tim! When did you put all this together?"

"That doesn't matter, but OMG, you said yes, that makes me so happy! I love you, Julissa Lucky. You are my missing piece. You have always been my missing piece!"As he kisses her with so much love.

Tim then says, "Babe, we have reservations at Buca Lupo. We will meet you allthere." He says to the crowd.

"What about dinner, here?"

"Well… that was a little lie to get you here tonight. Sorry,love, but I won't make that a habit."

"You better not." She says.

"Dinner is at 8:30, so we need to go." He says as they all leave for the restaurant.Lester even shows up.

Everyone arrives and eats an amazing dinner. Alex keeps looking at MamaLucky because he's not familiar with who she's with. Towards the end of dinner, Lester grabs a glass of wine and make a toast of thehappy couple.

"Who are you?" Alex asked.

"Oh, that's right. You two haven't met yet. Alex, Lester and Lester, Alex." she says as she points towards the both of them respectively.

'Okay, who is he though?" He says.

119

"Alex, let's talk about this later." Says mama Lucky.

'No, mom, let's do this now!" Alex says.

Julissa grabs Alex, and tries to calm him, which she does, but he is still making ascene.

"Baby brother, please not today."

As she walks up to him, and tries to get him to leave, or atleast go outside. Julissa persuades him, and he goes outside and they drive off.Mama Lucky and Lester then leave also. Dinner was over after all that, Julissa thought.

Julissa and Tim leave too, and go back to her suite. After everything just happened,she wants him to stay.

They then grab a few bottles of water and they go and get into bed and lay there for a while. Julissa stares at her ring, and says, "That was a great surprise, love. Ilove you, baby. I am so tired though, no nookie tonight, I hope you're not mad at me.Sorry, hopefully, Alex calms down though."

"Oh, no problem, baby." Tim says even though he wanted her so bad.

He decided to take a shower. They take off their clothes, and get up and get into theshower. While there, he tries to touch her, but she just wants to clean herself up, and get back into bed. Tim finishes up in the shower and also gets out and also getsback into bed

They start to cuddle and Julissa says, "Good night, baby. I love you." And they both hugeach other, and go to sleep.

Chapter 15

Kera's Trip Back to the A (Atlanta)

It is 5:30 A.M. when Julissa wakes up from the loud sirens blaring outside. She reached out and grabs her phone, seeing that it is a little earlier than she expected, she rolls back over to wait for her alarm to go off. She gets up after thirty minutes when her alarm goes off. First, she goes into the kitchen and starts the coffee pot. Then turns on the water to the shower as she gets her clothes out the closet. As she walks back into the bathroom the window to the shower is completely fogged up. She then gets in, and lets the steam moisturize her skin. She then gets in the hot water, and washes her body. She is in the shower for about20 minutes and then she finally gets out and dries herself off and puts her towel around her to do her hair.

Usually she puts it in curls but today she changed up. She first blow dried it, and then straightened it out. Her hair was getting longer, she thought. She finished up with her hair then went to the bedroom. While in the bedroom she grabs the lotionand lotions her entire body. She then grabs her clothes, and starts to get dressed. Today would be a long day so she decided to dress for comfort.

She decided to wear some flats rather than heels that would make her uncomfortable as she works. She decided on a dress today. A long dress with a cute blue jean vest, and flats. The dress was white with blue stripes. She grabs her white flats. Slips on her vest, and checks her hair one last time in the mirror, and walks out of the bedroom.

Looking at the clock, it was now about 7:15 checking her phone she sees an email from Mr. Prince. The Market will be coming in late. She quickly opens the email and it reads, Miss Lucky, can you please come and open up the building this morning, because due toa bit of an emergency I will not be available to open. So, please, open by 7:45 A.M. Thank you, see you a little later, if not, I will give you a call.

Julissa quickly grabs her Yeti pours her coffee, and wipesoff the cup before she grabs her bag and head downstairs to the lobby.

Once she gets to the lobby, she sees the front desk lady, and she asks her to get someone to clean her suite. It hadn't been cleaned thoroughly in a few weeks. It was not dirty, but just a bit of dust. Anyway, she sets that up and then leaves out thedoor, and as she is walking to her car, Big Joe drives up to wait for Dennis.

"Good morning, beautiful queen," says Big Joe as Julissa walks by.

"Oh, hey, Big Joe, good morning to you too."

"Thanks. Where is Dennis, because he's going to be late. He needs to make it in on time today. He should be out soon as well," says Big Joe.

"All right, then, I'm on my way there now."

"Have a good day! Got to go."

Just as she iswalking to her car, Dennis comes out!

"Good morning, boo." He says.

Julissa just ignores him, and gets in her car as if she hadn't heard him. Started her car, and hurries to get out of there. She figured she is going to see him in a little while anyway, so why deal with his man again now.

I'll see him at work in a few minutes. I need to get there to open up, she thought. She arrives, at work and opens up the door. She couldn't believe no one was there yet. She gets in, turns on the lights, go to her office, and puts up her things. She then goes to the conference room, and starts the coffee pot. Also goes to the break room to turn on the coffee pot in there also.

People start coming in, and going to their desk. After they turn on their computers, and head to the conference room for the daily briefing to start out the day. It is now a little behind schedule, but Julissa has a list of things she needs to discuss with all employees. She talks about assigned parking spots. Graphics deadline for this week's newsletter. Everyone starts asking where Mr. Prince is?

"Emergency!"

Jerome blurts out, "What emergency? I saw him out with some lady I know from the ship-strip club. Sounds to me like the emergency is him worn out and can't get his ass up and come to work on time, but I'm not one to gossip." Says Jerome.

Everyone laughs, and start talking, but Julissa quickly quiets everyone down. She speak of Mr. Michael's new job for the next few months.

"Few months? I thought Mr. Prince said, the rest of the year."

Julissa says, "Well, I don't have all the info yet, but I will be able to let you know that, for now, at least, prepare to be on flights." Says Julissa. Then she once again addresses everyone, "Okay, back to the announcements. We are starting an employee of the week pick. You will receive a $200 bonus, and a free lunch with Mr. Prince and myself. Well, that concludes the daily announcements. Have a great day, everyone."

When everyone gets back to work, Julissa goes back to her office as well and gets busy with her work, it is just then that she gets a call from Kera.

"Hey, boo. How are you today?" Ask Kera.

"Oh, I'm great over here. Question is how are you? How's Japan?"

"Oh, I'm not in Japan right now. We got on a flight to Florida last night. He had to be here to meet with another client, and I was with him, and we were having such a great time that we didn't want it to end." Says Kera.

"What the fuck? Are you serious? You just hopped another flight and you didn't say anything?"

"I'm fine, Julissa," says Kera.

"That is so irresponsible! I thought you were in Japan, and you are on the other side. Anyways, are you still coming home tonight?"

"Yes, our flight should be leaving at 8:00 P.M.," says Kera.

"That is extra late for a flight, but it will be great to see you." Says Julissa "And be so careful, girl!"

"I am. He has been so much fun. Such a gentleman. We had breakfast in bed this morning. It was delicious." She says.

"What part of Florida are you in? What hotel are you staying in? I need more details, boo. I'm upset you didn't tell me before now. Something could have happened, and I wouldn't have been able to know where to look." Says Julissa.

"Anyways, I am calling you now, so I just wanted you to know I am okay. I knowwe hadn't spoken much and I felt you needed me to call." She says.

"Thanks for calling. Love you, Kera. Can't wait to see you tonight. Oh, yeah. By theway we are at one of his homes. Here in Miami."

"Houses? Damn, Ki. How many houses does he have?" She asks.

"Well, never mind. I have to go anyway. Once you get ready for your flight, pleasegive me a call. I want to make sure I am up once you get here." Says Julissa.

"Okay, boo. Sure thing, bye for now." Says Kera

"Bye," and she hangs up.

Immediately after, "Miss Lucky, can I see you in my office?" Asks Mr. Prince who got to office while Julissa was on call.

"Sure, I am coming." Says Julissa.

"Did you do the morning announcements?" He asks.

"Yes, sir, I sure did. Everyone is here, and on board with everything. I spoke withthem all. Hope things are okay with you." Says Julissa.

"Okay. That is all I needed. You can go and finish what you were doing." He says."I thought you were on a call."

"Also, prepare Mr. Michaels for that campaign, ASAP. He is single, right? Because hewill always be around women. He has to make sure the products sell. One more thing, I hope you've cleared your schedule because as we've already discussed you will be going with him." Says Mr. Prince.

"Yes. I am working on it." She says.

"Okay, Missy. You will need to have an open schedule. Don't worry about anythingas usual we will take care of all of your expenses." He says, "That is all Ms. Lucky."

But just before she leaves, he says, "Will you be taking lunch today for work?"

"I'll probably have something delivered. What are we ordering for the staff today?

"Pizza, I think." He says.

"Oh, In that case, I might just grab a few slices of pizza and take it to my office." She says.

"Okay, so you don't need to leave today?" He asked.

"No, I don't." She says.

Julissa then goes back to her office, and starts going through her emails. She goesinto the new application file.

"We do need to hire about three more people for this season. There will be a lot more traffic coming through the mailroom, we need to hire one more photographerand the call center needs more. So, actually four more people" she thought out loud to herself. She thenreads a few applicants, and there is one name that really stood out to her in the photography department. Niecy Summers. Her resume was very impressive. She was a freelance photographer, and was moving to Atlanta.

Julissa quickly looks for a phone number to call her in for an interview. Looking down further realizing she will be moving in a week to Atlanta. Well she finds hernumber and then goes to speak about interviewing her to Mr. Prince.

She showed him her resume, and then they both agreed on calling her in for an interview. This girl had some beautiful pictures in the mini-portfolio she added in her resume, with a link to see more of her work. Julissa quickly checks out her other work, I figured this must be her full portfolio. She thought, she had so much experience, and really professional style photos.

Julissa quickly calls her.

As soon as she answers, Julissa introduces herself, "Hi, my name is Miss Lucky from Once, a magazine here in Atlanta, Georgia. I've taken a look at your job application and resume, and I would like to have you in for an interview. How about next week onFriday? You'll be here already, right?"

"Yes, I'm lucky. I will be moving in this week. I should be settled in, this waybefore Friday. I would be happy to come in for an interview."

"Okay, sounds great. So, next Friday? Which will be the 12th? So, we will see you onthe 12th at 8:00 A.M." says Julissa.

"8:00 A.M. sharp, Miss Lucky. Thank you so much."

"You're welcome, Miss Summers. I will be looking forward to meeting you." theyboth say goodbye and hang up.

Julissa walks back to Mr. Prince's office and tells him that she set up an interviewfor next week Friday.

"Okay, well that is great! I think she will be a real asset to the company." He says.

"Yes. I certainly agree with you, Mr. Prince. She has a lot of different photo ideas. She'sawesome! I cannot wait to see what idea she has for us." Says Julissa.

"Yes, well, if the interview goes good we will find out," he says.

'We shall." says Julissa.

"Well, I'm going to go up front and get some pizza. Would you like a few slices?"She asked.

"I am not hungry right now. Once I get hungry, I will go down and get something for myself, but thank you for asking," he says.

"Okay, then, I'll be back in a few minutes." She says.

"All right, no problem but here, can you please bring me a tea back out of themachine?" as he hands her twenty-five dollars.

"Sure, no biggie. I'll get it on my way back." She says.

"Yes, of course, that is fine." He says as she walks out the door into the front of thebuilding where the conference room was.

She walks in, and the table is full of a variety of different flavored pizza stacked together in boxes.

She saw the kind she wanted, added them to her plate, grabbed a soda from the cooler, andthen stopped by the Coke machine. She grabbed a tea for Mr. Prince then headedback to his and her office.

Just as she passes the other employees, Jerome walks by, and smiles, and says, "Good afternoon, Miss Lucky. How are you doing today? That pizza is extra good today."

"Iam glad, Mr. Jerome. You seem to be good, yourself."

"I am, Miss lucky. My girl had a girl last night." He says.

"Why are you not with your girl and new baby?" She asked.

"I was scheduled to work today. You know I don't like missing work. I saw her last night. She is such a beautiful little tiny little thing. I can't wait to get back there." Hesays.

"I'll talk to Mr. Prince, and see if you can leave a little earlier today. I didn't even know you had a girlfriend or baby on the way. You know we will give you a weekoff with pay. You just have to sign some papers but, yes we are not heartless. You should be there when that baby starts its life."

"Thank you. Hopefully, he says yes." Jerome says.

"I am sure he will. Family is important, and the employee of the week contest willnot start till next month."

"Okay, I thought I was going to miss my chance," he says.

"Oh, no, but if you miss more than a week you might need to come in. But you said youdon't like to miss much work, so I'm pretty sure you won't do that." She says.

"Yes, I feel like I'm missing something."

"Okay, now, I got to go, but I will come back with whatever he says." She walksaway.

She walks back to the office, puts her food on her desk, and then goes to Mr. Prince's office to give himhis tea.

"Thank you." He says.

"Oh, no problem, Mr. Prince, I was going there anyway," as she walked back to heroffice.

She sits down at her desk and eats her lunch while watching YouTube videos. Sheloves watching dance videos. She watches for about 20 minutes until Mr. Prince yells across the hall. "Now get back to work!"

Julissa then refreshes her computer, and gets back to applications. She pulls up the applications for the call center. She is skimming through the applications until she runs across this guy named Maxwell Fleming. It says he has worked at the eBay call Center for 10 years. She puts him tothe side, and continues with her search. As she was searching she got a text from Kera.

It reads: Hey, boo. How are you? Finally, I got a chance to text you. We are going to a Jay Zconcert next week in Atlanta. Jaleel is taking me. You're welcome to go if you like!

Julissa replies: Awesome. Kera, you are still coming tonight, right?

Yes, boo. Don't worry. I am enjoying myself with him but all he does is work. Plus, I need to get back to work by myself. Kera texts.

Yes, and I miss having you here. Julissa's text reads.

I know, boo. But I've got to begin spending time with him. I think we are good together. He works a lot but next time I won't be so far away. Okay, at least for afew months while we get to know each other. She texts back.

But we are about to board our flight. She texts again immediately after.

Okay, be careful. Have a safe flight. Love you,see you later. Julissa texts.

I will text you once we land. We have two stops, but the last one is atl. Kera texts back.

Then,got to go. Yay!

Julissa text back, TTYL.

Julissa gets back to her applications, and she reads through a couple more, and thencomes across a female Advocate by the name of Parker Guidry. She is very impressed once again, and grabs and puts it to the side. Just in case one of these falls through she looks through for a few more.

Looking at the clock, she sees it is now 2:45 P.M. almost time for her to go home and she starts to close things out, and takes out her trash, and straightens her desk abit. She takes a sip of her soda, and then quickly goes to the restroom. She had been holding it for quite some time, but now it was the last hour and she had to go. She finishes up in there, and then goes down the hall to make sure everyone is busy doing their work.

She walks past Jennifer's desk and says, "Hey, girl, did you finish the interview with Lady ATL? I need that on my desk first thing tomorrow morning. I need to proofread, and haveit typed up for Monday. Have a great weekend! I will give you a call on Sunday to check on that interview paperwork." Says Julissa.

"Oh, yes, Miss lucky. I will look through my notes of the interview, and have it foryou first thing Monday." Jennifer says.

"Oh, no, I said the first thing tomorrow." says Julissa.

"Oh, my bad, I meant tomorrow, you have a great weekend also."

"All right. That is your deadline. I can't give you any more days." She says.

On her way back from there, she saw Jerome walking to his desk. "Did you finish the editing for the photos of Mr. Michael's? I will need those at the close of your shift today. Also, is there any morepizza left?" Asks Julissa.

"Yes, I saw at least four boxes that were still left." Says Jerome.

"Why, thank you. I think I'm going to take a box home. No need to let it go to waste. I need to get rid of that pizza, you guys!" says Julissa to the entire floor. "But please,save a box for Mr. Prince."

Everyone said, "Okay, Miss Lucky."

She grabs a box and opens it. It was a pepperoni. She thought, I don't want that one. She opens another one, and it is a cheese. She quickly grabs it and takes it toher office, and puts it on her little table.

She looks back at the applications, and writes down the first two numbers. I willcall them before I leave today. She thought. Then she sits looking for a mailroom person. There are a few that she likes, but ofcourse, she has to show them to Mr. Prince before they come for an interview.

As she is getting up, there is a knock at the door, and it is the janitor, Beverly. She says, "Good afternoon, Miss Lucky, would you like me to take your trash, and dust things up a bit?

'Well, no to the trash. I already took that out myself, because it was kind of just trash from my lunch."

"Oh, no problem, I will just a little, and get on out of your hair." Says Beverly.

"Oh, well, thank you." says Julissa as she walks across the hall to Mr. Prince forhis opinion on the people she found.

She lays info on the desk and says, "I think these choices for the mailroom and callcenter will be great ones. I've looked over their experience, and it will certainly be an answer to the company." says Julissa.

"I need to make a phone call, and then we can discuss it a little more." says Mr. Prince.

"Okay, well, I'll come back. I'll be leaving in about an hour. I'll go check with thestaff to see who's ready for Monday's issue." Julissa says as she walks out of the office.

"Okay, sounds great." says Mr. Prince. "See you back here in 10."

"I'll be back." she says as she walks out.

Julissa goes back down the hall to check on the progress. It was almost time to go.On Fridays they left at 4:00 P.M. It was now 3:15, but she was leaving early today.

She talks to the staff, seeing that Jennifer has finished going over the paperwork,and hands it to her.

"Great job!" Jennifer says, "Way to go! You know how Mr. Prince hates last minuteprep."

"Yes, I know. It's not like me to be last minute, but I realize I needed to put a rush onit!"

"Very impressive work, Miss Jennifer, even with the broken arm you still can dowhat you're supposed to do well." She says.

"Thanks so much. I don't need a bad rep." She says.

"Okay, well, I see you are all keeping busy. Hopefully, everything is done today. If not, we may have to work a little later today. Oh, my bad, you all may have to worklater. I leave at 4:00 today."

Just then she gets a text from Kera. It says: I just landed a one and a half hour layover. Going to go get a bite to eat, and head to walk to the waiting area for theflight. Love you, see you soon.

Thanks for the update. I love you too. I'll give you a call once I get off. Julissa texts back.

Okay, bye. Kera says in a text back.

"All right, you guys, good progress, love your extra effort to finish before thedeadline today."

On her way out, she does one last check, than she walks on back to her office.Looking over at Mr. Prince to see if he is off the phone waiting on her, so she stopped in.

"It is a yes for me for all three candidates, and if need be, the others can be on standby, and called if necessary, but definitely yes on the three. A great choice, Miss Lucky.Now I know, why I made you my VP, you are always thinking in the company's best interest."he says.

127

"I thank you, Mr. Prince. It is great to be appreciated," she says.

"Well, it's great to have someone to appreciate," he says.

"Wow, Mr. Prince, you are in a great mood today! Throwing around all of thesecompliments. What has gotten into you?" Asks Julissa.

"What are you saying? I am always nice, Miss Lucky. I can't believe you asked methat!" he says.

"No, not like this. You must be seeing a new lady or something. You laying it on extra thick today! I haven't seen you with your teeth this much since I started here."she says.

"Oh my, I can't believe your accusations, I'm always smiling. Anyways, go call these people, and set up interviews, please, then go home. You're not trying to work OT, areyou?"

"Oh, no, I have things to do. I'll go make those calls, and then go home. Bye Mr.Prince. Have a great weekend, but something tells me you already plan to."

"Out! Miss lucky!" He yells.

"Okay. I'm going."

She says as she then leaves his office and goes to hers, and callsthe people. Once done, she hurriedly leaves the office to finally go home.

When she gets home, Tim calls and asks her to dinner. She takes the offer, and goesto shower.

It's funny, I can't believe that no one asked me about my ring, she thought as she admires her beautiful diamond ring!

She gets in and takes a quick shower, then gets out and looks for the best set of undergarments. Straight to the lingerie drawer, she finds a really pretty pink bra and panty set with a garter belt.

Thinking, I'm sure I'll be staying tonight. She grabs a nice white clingy little dress and some heels, and goes to put on a little makeup. Herhair was still good from the day because she put her cap on during her shower. So, that was already done.

Tim calls again, and asks, "Do you want to come to my suite or yours?"

She says, "I'll come to yours. I still need to do a few things before I'm ready to go."

"We have a reservation at 6:30, love." He says.

"Well, I guess I'm comingnow. I'm dressed, I just need to put on my shoes, and grab a light jacket. My outfit needs one." She says.

"Oh, see you in a few." He says.

She grabs a jacket and her bag, and heads to Tim's suite.

As he opens the door. He is mesmerized, "Damn, baby, white? You know you areworking that dress! Looks like that booty has gotten a bit bigger, too." he says.

"Really, babe?" She says.

"Why, yes! Makes me want to skip dinner and eat you instead. Yum yum," He says.

'No, I want to go and eat." she says.

"Oh, we are going, I was just so excited at the sight of you in that dress, and I kind ofoverreacted"

"Okay, let's go." She says.

They both go downstairs, into the car and drive on to the restaurant. The reservations were a restaurant a little farther, but finally they got there. They go in the restaurant, which is in a totally secluded area of Atlanta. It was called Perry's Steakhouse.

Julissa looks at the time, it was now 6:23 P.M. They park the car and get out of it to go inside. The tables were covered in white cloth with a gold 10-piece. The walls were black with gold designs. This place was exquisite. The glasses had gold trim, same with the plates. The waitresses were dressed in all black attire. They sat at their assigned table and looked at the menu for a while.

Julissa then gets a text from Kera: Loading for flight. Should land by 9:00. It's like a two and a half hour flight.

Okay, Ki. Sounds great! I can't wait to see you. She texts back.

There are some technical difficulties and they are now having us to get off the plane. So now it will probably be a longer wait. Kera replies.

Oh, okay, well, we are at dinner right now. I will text you back once we are done to see if you have left yet, or you can just text me once y'all leave. Julissa texts.

Where are you, by the way? You never said.

Oh, don't be mad, but we are still in Florida. We missed our first flight.

We are now about to get on a flight directly to Georgia. Kera texts.

Okay, whatever. I'll talk to you about that later, but for now keep me posted when you are leaving. Julissa texts.

Okay, Julissa, talk to you soon. Kera replies.

Julissa checks the menu, and then the waitress comes back and they both order, enjoy some conversation, and a great dinner. They stay for quite a while. They dance, and truly enjoy themselves and then go back to Tim's place.

At 10:30, Kera sends text: Loading now. It's going to be a one and a half hour flight. We should land at 12:00 A.M.

Julissa text back: Okay, I'll be at Tim's.

Okay, great! Glad you're not alone.

Tim decides to start a movie, and they sit and watch. He offers her a glass of wine and she declines, because she had too much at dinner.

About 2 hours go by and it is 12:30 A.M.

Julissa calls Kera, but no answer, it goes straight to voicemail. Her texts yielding the same results, nothing.

She turns on the news and realizes that a plane on the way to Atlanta got into some bad weather, and lost control due to going off course, and crashed somewhere off the coast.

"Oh my god! No, no, no!" She screams. "Kera's plane went down!"

She woke up Tim because he had fallen asleep during the movie. Again, she calls Kera's phone with no answer! She keeps calling but it always goes to voicemail.

"I told her that trip was a bad idea and now look! Babe, I will not sleep till I know something. This is terrible! I hope she's okay. Imean, are they okay?"

It is now 12:45 A.M., she flips to the news to see if she can find out anything. While watching, a fresh new bulletin comes up and it says a plane went off course and is nowmissing somewhere. Now, understanding a little more, but still absolutely terrified, Julissa calls Kera's phone again, but still nothing!!

"Oh my God,maybe, she didn't get on the plane," she suggests to Tim.

"Well, I know a few people at the airport, babe. Maybe, I can get some answers ashe walks off to go call someone…

www.ingramcontent.com/pod-product-compliance
Lightning Source LLC
Chambersburg PA
CBHW080833250626
47160CB00008B/2917